What Do
We Do Now,
George?

What Do We Do Now, George?

Helen McCann
Illustrated by Ellen Eagle

SIMON & SCHUSTER BOOKS FOR YOUNG READERS

Published by Simon & Schuster
New York • London • Toronto • Sydney • Tokyo • Singapore

SIMON & SCHUSTER BOOKS FOR YOUNG READERS

Simon & Schuster Building, Rockefeller Center, 1230 Avenue of the Americas,
New York, New York 10020. Text copyright © 1989 by Helen McCann.
Illustrations copyright © 1991 by Ellen Eagle. All rights reserved including
the right of reproduction in whole or in part in any form. Originally published
in Great Britain by Macdonald Children's Books. First U.S. edition 1991.
SIMON & SCHUSTER BOOKS FOR YOUNG READERS is a trademark of Simon & Schuster.

Designed by Lucille Chomowicz.
The text of this book is set in Baskerville.
The illustrations were done in pencil.
Manufactured in the United States of America.   10   9   8   7   6   5   4   3   2   1

Library of Congress Cataloging-in-Publication Data McCann, Helen. What do we
do now, George?/Helen McCann: illustrated by Ellen Eagle.   p.   cm.
Summary: Thirteen-year-old George's plans to raise money for his school and keep
a percentage for himself create chaos and get him in trouble with his friends and
the authorities. [1. Moneymaking projects—Fiction.   2. Schools—Fiction.
3. Humorous stories.]   I. Eagle. Ellen, ill.   II. Title.   PZ7.M1244Wh   1991
[Fic]—dc20   91-2329 CIP ISBN: 0-671-74688-X

For Stephen and Matthew

George looked at the skateboard. It was the most beautiful thing he had ever seen—apart from Sharon Taylor. And it didn't look at him as if he had just crawled out from under a rock the way Sharon Taylor did. It just sat there in the shop window, begging to be bought. It wasn't the old-fashioned kind either, so thin that your feet hung over the edge. It was broad and curved at the front with a tail at the back and smooth-running wheels. It had tiny little fins just above the back trucks. Aerodynamic, thought George. Perfect.

His birthday had been three months ago and Christmas was not for another six months yet. He hadn't a snowball's chance of getting it. He ran a hand through the sandy hair that always flopped over his forehead no matter what he did to it.

"Great, isn't it?" said a voice behind him, and up about five inches. Paul Graham, also known as Stick, had put in a lot of growing since he had turned thirteen, mostly in the legs. He reminded George of a stick insect and walked with a sort of bounce, as if he hadn't gotten used to his height yet.

"Hi, Stick," said George.

They had been friends since kindergarten. Four of them had hung out together. George, Stick, Tub Robson, and Kev Chisholm.

"They're running a contest for one of those," said Stick, looking at the skateboard.

"Contests are a mug's game," said George. "They're always fixed beforehand. How much does it cost to enter?"

"It's free," said Stick. "All you have to do is think up a name for it."

"You mean like *Styler* or *Transmission*?" said George.

"Suppose so." Stick shrugged. "Anyway, I've entered. I mean, it's free. Why not?"

"Advertising stunt," said George. "You'll never win." But he went into the store anyway, just to get a better look at the skateboard. The entry forms were lying in a pile on top of the counter.

"What name did you think up?"

"*Asteroid Two*," said Stick. "Good, eh?"

George looked at him.

"Why *Two*?"

He shrugged.

"I don't know. It just sounded good."

George was filling in his name and address on an entry form, just to pass the time. Well, it was free, wasn't it?

"We'll have to get a move on or we'll be late," said Stick. "What have you got first period?"

George looked at the blank on the form that said "write your suggestion here."

"Classical background."

"Boring," said Stick. "I tell you, last week it was all about some horse that could fly—I had no idea what old Burns was talking about."

"Lives in a world of his own," said George. "Latin and stuff. I mean, hardly anybody in the school takes it. Dead languages—what's the point? I mean, how many ancient Romans are you going to meet on High Street?"

"I've got economics—double period," said Stick. "So hurry up. Turnbull's not happy if you're late."

George scribbled down the first thing that came into his head and shoved the form through the slot in a box on the counter.

"Economics is the thing," he said, following Stick out of the shop. "Learning how to get rich quick."

"Huh," said Stick. "If it's so easy, how come Turnbull's teaching us and not living it up in some tax haven enjoying his millions?"

"You need flair," said George. "Turnbull's got no imagination, no ideas."

"Some people get too many ideas," said Stick, "naming no names, of course."

George ignored that.

"You need ideas," he said. "You have to take chances, risks. You have to look at the market and see where the need is."

"Oh, yeah, like selling homework answers and getting them wrong?" said Stick.

George took a swipe at him with his school bag.

"That was French," he said. "I never said I was any good in French."

"And what about the candy apples? It cost you more than you made to get that stuff to clean your mom's stove."

"Okay, so I haven't hit on the right scheme yet," said George dreamily. "But when I do . . . when I do . . ."

"Pigs will fly," said Stick as they turned in at the school gates, "or you'll meet an ancient Roman on High Street."

George was always dreaming up schemes to get rich quick. Ever since Stick had known him, George had been full of crazy ideas. Even in elementary school. It was his hobby, like some people made model airplanes. They all had some kind of mania, Stick thought. Take Tub Robson. With him it was food. And Kev—his was wildlife and conservation and things. Last year it had been saving the whales and a few months ago it was the big old oak trees they were going to cut down to make room for the new supermarket parking lot.

The trouble with Kev was he went too far at times. Anyway, he chained himself to one of the trees and threw the key to the padlock away. Eventually the fire department had to cut him loose. Still, he made his point. It got in the local paper and the Friends of the Earth or somebody got involved and the trees were saved. The parking lot had to be moved to another site and Kev got a social worker. He was furious at the time—kept asking why he had to have a social worker—till he met her.

She was interested in plants and that kind of stuff and was helping him to start a wild garden. Knowing Kev, wild was about right. But then his dad had given his mom this garden gnome and now she wanted to build a patio over Kev's wild garden. His mom didn't call it a wild garden though—she called it a patch of weeds. Poor Kev. That gnome was trouble and Kev really hated it.

As for Stick himself, he had enough to worry about keeping out of his sister Julia's way. And then there was that dog his mom had bought. Stick couldn't make up his mind which was worse—Julia or the dog. Probably the dog. At least his dad wasn't always nagging him to take Julia for a walk.

Or maybe Stick's dad was worst of all. Dads were a terrible hassle. That's where George was lucky. He hadn't ever had a dad. Maybe that was why he was so bossy—being just him and his mom. He got away with murder. His mom never yelled at him even when he did crazy things. Usually she just laughed and said he would grow up soon enough. And that made George wild.

"See you," said Stick.

George didn't hear him. In fact, classical background came and went without George noticing. So did morning break. Wheels had begun to turn. He really wanted that skateboard.

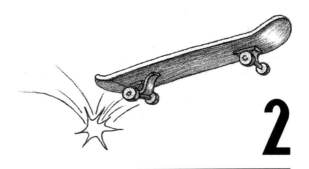

2

Halfway through French George realized he was on the wrong page of the book. Not that it made much difference. French was a mystery to him.

Mr. Martin, the French teacher, asked him a question.

"Sorry, Mr. Martin. I've lost the page," he said.

The teacher's face took on a resigned expression, the kind George was used to seeing on his mother's face. Like last week, when he tried setting up a business weeding gardens—with her vacuum cleaner. He had seen this commercial on TV for some machine that sucked up weeds and grass. He still couldn't understand why you couldn't just use an ordinary vacuum cleaner, except that it hadn't worked. He wondered if his mother would get a new one. He wondered if they could afford a new one.

"Find the page," Mr. Martin was saying patiently.

George dived headfirst into the gym bag at his feet.

Mr. Martin spoke again, louder this time.

"George. What are you doing?"

"Looking for the page, sir," he said.

Mr. Martin was pretty nice—for a teacher. He didn't throw chalk or erasers, and he wasn't the boring, sarcastic type either, like a lot of teachers. But even George could see he was really hanging on to his temper—like Tub Robson and the last cream puff in the universe.

"Are you trying to be funny?" he said.

Just for once, George wasn't.

"No, sir," he said.

"Then find the correct page."

He made another move toward the bag.

"*Aitken,*" thundered Mr. Martin. "I shall lose my patience with you soon. Will you find the page in your book!"

Light dawned at last on George.

"It's not in the book," he said. "When I said I had lost the page, I meant it was missing, not there, lost. I thought it might have fallen out into my bag." He spoke slowly, to make sure the teacher understood.

Some teachers were really thick. Not Mr. Martin though—at least, not usually. He must be having a rough day, thought George.

Mr. Martin walked slowly toward him. He reached down and picked up George's book. A few pages drifted loose and floated to the floor.

"How long has this book been in this state?" he asked. His voice was quiet.

"Since I got it," said George.

"And was the page there when you got the book?"

George blinked. What a stupid question.

"I don't know," he said. "They all look the same to me. I mean, they're in French."

He looked around at the rest of the class. The other students were grinning. None of them was good at French. Mr. Martin's face had gone pale. He looked as if he was trying to say something, but his mouth wasn't cooperating. He reached out a hand to George. George noticed that it was quivering slightly. Then the bell rang and the class was in an uproar as they stampeded for the door. George flung the book into his bag and began to gather up the loose pages. He stuffed them in and, when he glanced up, he saw Mr. Martin over by the window looking out. George stood there for a moment, watching the teacher. He was grinding stubs of chalk to dust on the window ledge.

"Nervous breakdown," said Kev Chisolm in George's ear. "Seen all the signs before. My dad went just like that when I dropped the gnome through the roof of the garden shed."

George's interest was immediately caught. "You never told me about that. What did you have against the garden shed?"

Kev punched him casually on the elbow, and George winced.

"The garden shed was an accident," he said. "It was the gnome I was trying to smash. I hate that gnome."

He turned to George, emotion showing clearly in his face, which was unusual. Kev usually looked kind of stunned—like a gorilla who had walked into a door.

"I got it all the way up to the roof," he said. "It wasn't easy, you know. Then it slipped the wrong way and fell through the roof. I meant to push it off and smash it on the rock garden. Still, it doesn't look too great anymore." He swaggered off down the corridor, kicking people lightly as he went.

Don't suppose the garden shed does either, thought George.

It was the latest thing with Kev—this gnome his dad had gotten for the garden. Kev had gotten it into his head that if it weren't for the gnome, his mom wouldn't want this patio and he could keep his wild garden. Even though he was a clumsy guy, he was great with plants and things. His solution to the problem was simple—destroy the gnome. They had all had to listen to him talk about it for weeks now. One thing you could say for Kev, George thought, when he got on to a subject, he stuck with it.

Speaking of sticking with a subject, George began to wonder if he could persuade the gym teacher to buy skateboards as gym equipment. He could imagine the answer he would get if he asked. *This school can't even buy books and you're asking for skateboards.* Maybe it was thinking that or maybe it was the French book or even having to share a math book with Tub, but something began to stir deep in George's mind. Tub was crunching hard candies, which drowned out the sound of the teacher's voice and left him with a mind free to ponder. It came to him that his class was sharing an awful lot of tacky

textbooks these days. He had even heard teachers talking about it recently. But then, teachers were always complaining about something. It wasn't as if they expected you to notice.

It was later, when he was lining up to use the Bunsen burner in chemistry, that the idea came to him. That was the great thing about ideas. If you left your mind open long enough, they just sort of arrived there. Teachers never appreciated that. They were always nagging you about not paying attention. Einstein probably had the same problem when he was at school. Kev had George by the lapel at the time, asking him if he thought the chemistry teacher would suspect anything if he asked her what acid would do to concrete.

"How many Bunsen burners do we have in this lab, Kev?" said George.

Kev's brows drew together. "Who wants to know?" he said.

George sighed. Kev wasn't really tough. He just liked to act tough. It was the way he looked. People expected him to be tough.

"Just count them, Kev. I can't see past you."

Kev turned and George lurched slightly as the fist that held his lapel clenched in concentration.

"Eight," he said.

George pondered. Eight, and twenty-four pupils in the class.

"Well, what do you think?" said Kev.

"What about?" said George.

"The gnome and the acid," said Kev.

George looked up at him. "Sounds like a horror movie," he said.

"Eh?" said Kev.

George unclamped the fist from his lapel.

"Look, why don't you convert a Bunsen burner into a blowtorch and try that on the gnome?"

He should have known better. A light appeared in Kev's eyes.

"You know, George, I don't care what anybody says about you and your nutty ideas. You've got brains." And he shouldered his way casually to the head of the line.

There wasn't time for George to have a turn on one of the Bunsen burners, and as they left the lab he looked around the benches.

Seven, he said to himself. I thought Kev said eight.

Kev was just going out the door. There was a length of rubber tubing hanging out of his blazer pocket.

"Keep trying, Kev," shouted George after him. "Eventually that gnome will die of embarrassment."

"You okay?" said Stick behind him.

"I've had an idea," said George.

Stick groaned. He should have known. He'd seen the signs.

"Is that the time?" he said, making a break for

freedom. But speed wasn't his thing. Height was his thing.

George grabbed him. "The park tonight. At the fountain. Seven-thirty. Tell anybody else you see."

"I have to take the dog for a walk."

"Bring the dog," said George.

"I think I might be coming down with bubonic plague."

"Fight it," said George. He was used to feeble excuses.

"Julia will want to come," said Stick, and held his breath. There was silence. Julia was eleven years old and had been poison ever since they were kids. She tried to tag along no matter what you said to her. You could say anything to her and she still didn't go away. George knew. George had been trying it for years.

"I'll think of something," said George.

"It's no good," said Stick. "She's like a blood-hound. You're wasting your time. She says she's going to be a newspaper reporter."

Julia was a pain in the neck. Julia was always butting in where she wasn't wanted. Julia just kept on and on till you noticed her, and most people would do anything, say anything, promise anything to get rid of her. Julia would be a really good newspaper reporter.

George brightened. "That's it," he said. "Publicity. We'll need publicity. Bring Julia."

Stick looked at him, stunned. "Sorry, George. I thought you said 'bring Julia.'"

"I did," said George.

Stick looked at him closely.

"Are you all right?"

"Bring Julia," said George.

Stick shook his head.

"I'm in shock," he said. "Nobody's ever said that to me—bring Julia. And now you've said it—twice." He bounced off, shaking his head sadly. "It's the end of civilization as we know it. The dog's better company than Julia."

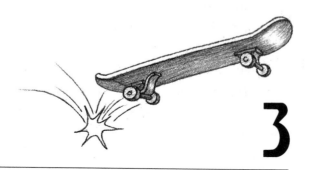

George arrived first. He was sitting on the low wall that surrounded the ornamental pond, throwing stones at the fountain in the middle. It was a favorite thing with him, mainly because of the horrible statue of a simpering cherub that stood on top of the fountain. Every so often a stone would glance off a passing duck, but mostly he got the cherub square between the eyes. He noticed a furry black thing bobbing along the top of the hedge on the opposite side of the pond. Sure enough, in a minute Stick bounced into view. An empty dog leash dangled from one hand.

"Where's Julia?" said George.

"She wouldn't come," said Stick. "She thought it was a trap."

"What kind of trap?"

Stick shrugged and bounced at the same time. It was positively balletic. "I don't know what kind of trap, but you can't blame her. I could hardly get the words out. I mean—asking her to come?"

"She must have thought you were acting suspiciously," said George.

"I was," said Stick. "It was weird."

George looked at the dangling leash. "Did the dog think it was a trap too?" he said.

Stick looked around wildly.

"It was there a minute ago. If I've lost it, I'll get killed. Mom got it only last week. It's a pedigree."

"A pedigree what?"

"Dog. What do you think?" said Stick.

Sometimes Stick was as bad as Kev.

"Why don't you just call it?" said George.

"Call it what?"

George had a sudden picture of Mr. Martin grinding chalk into dust. No wonder—he had to put up with this kind of thing for a living.

"Its name," said George.

"I can't remember its name," Stick said, trying to set off in all directions at once. He always looked as if he had more than his fair share of arms and legs. "It's one of those huge long things."

"What, the dog?" said George.

Stick looked at him.

"No, idiot, the name. The dog's insignificant. Don't you ever listen?"

"I've been listening. It doesn't seem to work," said George. "Look, what do you usually call it?"

"Bozo," said Stick.

"Yell Bozo, then," said George.

"That wouldn't do any good," Stick said. "It doesn't answer to Bozo."

The stone lay, tempting, in George's hand. He laid it down carefully on the wall beside him. He couldn't afford to kill Stick. Not just yet anyway. He might need him.

At that moment a small, hairy object shot out of the hedge. Stick sort of collapsed on top of it and clamped the collar around its neck. The dog looked a bit dazed.

Tub was the next to arrive. "I just stopped off at McDonald's on the way down," he said.

"Didn't you get any dinner at home?" said Stick. Even though he was as thin as a rake, he was as interested in food as Tub was.

"Mom's put me on a diet," said Tub.

Stick looked shocked. "That's cruelty to children," he said. "You should do something about that."

"I am doing something," said Tub. "I'm going to McDonald's."

"Social worker," said a voice, and they all jumped, even the dog.

Like a lot of big people, Kev could move really quietly.

"That's what you need, Tub," he said, pummeling Tub's stomach. "They're great. Mine got me more pocket money. Said I needed—what was it now?" His brow furrowed with effort. It was painful to watch. "The chance to explore the limits of my responsibilities. How about that, then?"

He was really pleased with himself.

"And have you," said Stick, "gotten to the limit, I mean?"

"Dad says I have," said Kev, looking not at all bothered.

Tub was staring. There was something even odder-looking than usual about Kev. It was a minute before George realized his eyebrows were missing.

"Hi, Kev," he said. "What happened to your eyebrows?"

Kev's massive hand shot up to the place where his eyebrows had been.

"Singed off," he said.

"Accident, was it?" said Tub, rubbing his stomach. You could tell he thought it served Kev right and why stop at the eyebrows.

Kev nodded. "Not that I'm blaming George," he said. George nearly fell into the pond from fright. "It was a great idea making a blowtorch, but I don't think I got the connection right."

"What connection?" said Stick.

"On the propane tank," said Kev. "It's been sitting outside all winter and the label had come off."

They were all staring at him.

"Anyway, no harm done," said Kev. "The trailer's not a total writeoff and the social worker is there again. She's talking about getting somebody to come and see Dad. Says he needs help."

There was silence. They all stood looking at Kev. Maybe it was the absence of eyebrows. In most people an eyebrow here or there might not be missed, but in Kev's case they had added a certain something to his face. Without them he looked like one of those Easter Island statues they had seen a film about in art history. They could hear the rhythmic thud of tennis balls on the courts behind the hedge. George couldn't stand the strain any longer.

"Okay, I give in. Where does the trailer fit into the picture?"

Ken grinned.

"The gas tank was attached to the trailer," he said.

Talking to Kev was like playing a slot machine. You had to get the combination right.

"Was the trailer still there when you left?" said George.

Kev scratched his head.

"Some of it," he said.

George gave up. He didn't have time for chitchat. He looked around at the little group. Stick and Tub were staring at Kev in a glazed kind of way that might have been admiration. The dog was whimpering as well as it could, which wasn't much because Tub was standing on its leash and its head was on the ground gasping for air. Stick yanked the leash from under Tub's feet, the dog yelped, and the spell was broken.

"Right," said George. "Gather around. I've had this idea."

Stick groaned. "I thought you might have forgotten about that."

"You don't know what it is yet," said George.

"I'd like to keep it that way," said Stick. "The last time you had an idea, I got my pocket money stopped for a month."

"Get a social worker," said Kev. "They're great for pocket money." Kev was always talking about his social worker, trying to make everyone jealous. Sometimes George wondered if he got into trouble on purpose just so that they wouldn't take his social worker away. At any rate, he never seemed to mind getting into trouble and he got along really well with her.

"Look," said George. "Just listen to it. That can't do any harm."

They didn't look convinced. George had a brainstorm.

"Tell you what," he said. "Listen to the idea and if you don't think it's the best yet, you can chuck me in the pond."

Tub thought of all George's other ideas. "It wouldn't have to be very good to be the best yet," he said.

Stick was looking almost cheerful. "It's worth the risk," he said. "You promise now? We really can chuck you in the pond?"

"Scout's honor," said George.

"You haven't been a scout since you demagnetized the Kestrel Patrol's compass before they did their orienteering badge," said Tub.

George sighed. Tub was always harping on his past. "They all got their survival skills badge out of it, didn't they?"

"I was in the cubs once," said Kev.

"That's impossible," said Stick. "They don't make the uniforms that big."

"I didn't have a uniform," said Kev. "I was in it only one week."

"What happened?" said Tub.

"They gave me all my badges and said I could leave the cubs and join the scouts when I was old enough."

"What cubs did you go to?" said Tub, interested. The only badge he had ever gotten was in cooking.

"The hut down by the common," said Kev.

"There isn't a hut down by the common," said Stick.

Kev grinned. "There used to be," he said.

Nobody asked what Kev had done to the hut.

George leapt off the wall, brushing the dog lightly with his foot. It yowled.

"Now, listen up. Be quiet and listen," he roared.

Tub looked offended. "You don't have to get mad," he said. "We were only waiting till you were ready."

"I'm ready. I'm ready," yelled George.

He settled once more on the wall. The dog cowered.

"You know how teachers are always going on about not having enough books or equipment—blaming the government, the education system, us even?"

Nods all around. They all knew the feeling. Half an hour's lecture when you got a book you didn't even want in the first place.

"Well then," said George. "How about starting a scheme to raise money? Think about it. Who could refuse? It's a good cause. What we have to do is think up a few projects. We'll need publicity. We can do all the usual things—sponsored walks and rummage sales and maybe come up with a couple of original ideas as well. We'll make a fortune."

They all had the same strange expression on their faces. George couldn't quite place it, but he thought it might be hate.

"For schoolbooks?" said Stick as if he couldn't believe his ears.

"You're right, Stick," said Tub. "It was a lousy idea.

What are we waiting for? Let's throw him in the pond."

They advanced on him slowly, silently, menacingly.

"Wait. Wait, I'm not finished," said George.

"That's what you think," said Stick.

He tried to back away—difficult since he was sitting on the edge of the pond. Even the dog was baring its teeth at him. He looked at it, hypnotized, then suddenly it keeled over and lay on its side, dead. Well, well, thought George. I didn't know I had it in me. What a talent.

Someone spoke from the other side of the pond. "Why, George, I think that's a wonderful idea."

They all froze—except for the dog. It wasn't doing much anyway.

"Oh, no," said Tub.

"Not her," said Stick.

If Kev had still had his eyebrows, they would have been drawn closely together.

George's voice got all gummed up, as if he'd just swallowed a rubber banana.

"Hello, Sharon," he said, looking stupid.

She was wearing a tennis skirt and white T-shirt and her long blond hair stirred gently in the breeze. She looked like a shampoo ad. She smiled at George, and he nearly fell in the pond without any help. It was so unexpected. They had been doing the

genetic scale in biology, and George figured that Sharon rated him around toad level. He didn't see the look of hopelessness that passed between Tub and Stick. Kev was looking like King Kong with a toothache.

Sharon floated toward him, swinging her tennis racquet. "Has anyone seen a tennis ball?" she said. "I'm afraid I misjudged that last shot a little." She giggled and Stick shuddered.

"Oh, there it is," she said, pouncing on it. "But what's wrong with your little dog? Is he asleep?"

George preened. "I seem to have killed it," he said. "I must have the power, like in that film about the guy that brings down buildings just by looking at them."

"You're thinking of Kev and scout huts," said Tub.

"No I'm not," said George.

Stick noticed the dog for the first time. After all, he was a long way up and the dog hadn't been saying anything.

"You killed the dog?" he yelled. "What did it ever do to you?"

"It was threatening me," said George, "like the rest of you."

"You stood on it," said Stick. "How would you like to be stood on?"

George thought he was about to find out, but Sharon was between them, bending over the dog.

"I don't think it's dead," she said, "just stunned.

The tennis ball must have hit it."

Stick was pulling wildly at his hair. "What am I going to say when I get home with a concussed dog? It might be in a coma. It might live on and on like that for years. I might have to look after it."

Sharon looked up at him with scorn in her blue eyes. "Oh, don't be ridiculous, Paul," she said. "It's coming around already."

Stick looked relieved, then another thought struck him. "What if it's brain damaged?"

George looked at the dog. It rolled its eyes drunkenly at him.

"How could you tell?" he said. "It wasn't that smart in the first place. I mean, it can't have much of a built-in early-warning system if it lets itself get hit with tennis balls. I thought dogs were supposed to have an instinct for danger."

"If you had any instinct for danger, you wouldn't still be sitting there," said Stick. You could tell he didn't know whether to attack George or see if the dog was okay. The dog won. He bent down and hauled it to its feet. It looked around vaguely and lay down again. Stick began talking to it frantically. George ignored him.

"I'll have to go and finish my match," said Sharon, "but I must say I admire you, George. I never thought you had it in you to do something like this."

For the first time George thought he might be getting somewhere with Sharon.

"I didn't really kill the dog," he said. "Remember?"

She shook her head impatiently. "No, no. I mean the project. Come over after school tomorrow. I'll have had some ideas by then."

She smiled at him as she turned away.

"You can listen to me practice my cello."

George was struck dumb. It was too much.

"Right," said Tub as Sharon disappeared around the hedge. "Let's throw him in the pond. Come on, Kev."

George found his voice. He hadn't told them the most important thing yet.

"Percentage," he yelled.

"Eh?" said Kev.

"Percentage," George repeated. "You don't think we're going to do this for nothing, do you? It's the way charities work — percentage for this, percentage for that. If you're good at it, you hardly have to give any of it away."

"My mom says that's a scandal," said Tub. "Making money out of good causes."

"Only if you're not the one getting the percentage," said George.

Tub nodded. "I can see that," he said.

Kev seemed to have missed the point. Probably because he was still on fractions.

"Back off, Kev," said Tub as Kev continued to approach George. "Let's hear the rest."

"What about the dog?" said Stick. "He deserves to be thrown in the pond for the dog's sake."

"It had nothing to do with me," said George. "It was the tennis ball."

Stick looked puzzled. "It feels as if it's your fault," he said.

"Everything always feels as if it's my fault," said George.

A voice spoke.

"I want my cut."

They all looked around.

"Did you hear that?" said George.

"It came from the hedge," said Tub. They looked at the hedge. It was a tall, loose kind of hedge. Good for pushing people into. A figure began to emerge slowly. It looked a bit like a matchstick with mange. Bits of hedge stuck up from its short curly hair. It was Julia.

"I want my cut," she said again. "And if you don't let me in on it, I'll tell Sharon Taylor what you're really up to."

George pondered. She really would be good at publicity, and she really would go running to Sharon.

"Okay," he said, making his voice sound grudging. It wasn't that hard when you were talking to Julia. "You're in—so long as you don't tell Sharon."

She looked a bit thrown by that, as if it had been too easy. Then she smiled.

"Called your bluff, didn't I?"

"Eh?" said George.

"You thought if you asked me to come, I would stay away."

George sighed. Julia was as straight as a corkscrew. He threw a last stone at the cherub and thought it rocked a bit on its pedestal.

"I'll need to take the dog home," said Stick. "I don't think it's well."

People stared at them as they trooped out of the park. They were an odd-looking bunch—Kev minus his eyebrows and Julia with bits of hedge sticking out of her hair like camouflage. But it was definitely the dog that got the old-lady-out-for-a-walk sympathy vote as it wavered uncertainly at the end of its leash. All in all, it hadn't been the dog's day.

As they passed through the park gates, Julia said, "There was a fire engine at your house when I went by, Kev."

Nobody mentioned the trailer.

George, for one, was busy. He was trying to work out how much they would have to make to get a percentage big enough (divided by five) to pay for the skateboard. Whichever way he looked at it, the number seemed to be the wrong way around.

"Have you done your homework?" asked his mother when he got in.

"Oh, Mom," said George. "What's the point?"

"The point is, you won't get into college if you don't pass your exams."

The way George looked at it, he would do better to get a job and then his mother wouldn't have to work so hard. She said she enjoyed working, meeting people in the store, but she got tired sometimes being on her feet all day, especially when she did overtime.

George went to do his homework, just to keep his mother happy. Time enough to fight the battle when he was old enough to quit school. That was the only thing about his mom—wanting him to stay in school. Apart from that she was okay—for a mom.

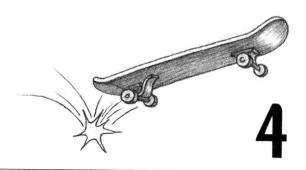

4

The next day George hung around after French. Mr. Martin was collecting books. It didn't take long. There weren't that many of them. He seemed to be a bit more normal today. He was piling the books into a low cabinet as George came up behind him.

"Mr. Martin?"

"Ugh!" The teacher raised his head too quickly, banging it on the cabinet door.

"Oh, Aitken," he said. "What are you doing here? The bell's rung."

"I just wanted to ask you something," said George.

Mr. Martin straightened up and kicked the door shut.

"The answer's no," he said, "but I suppose you want to ask anyway."

George ignored that. He'd heard it so often.

"You know this school has hardly any books," he said. "And the ones it has are a mess. And look at the equipment—Bunsen burners and things. Calculators, for instance," he added, thinking of the addition he couldn't do. "It's a disgrace."

"Good Lord," said Mr. Martin. "And there I was thinking you popped in only to pass the time between acts of vandalism."

"Oh, come on, sir," said George. "You know I'm not a vandal."

Mr. Martin rubbed his head. "Okay, George. It must have been the bump on the head. Still, you must admit, you're not in the school choir."

"What's that got to do with anything?" asked George.

"It is indicative of a certain sort of attitude," said Mr. Martin.

"Eh?" said George.

"Forget it. What did you want to ask me?"

George put the idea to him as clearly as he could. He didn't mention the percentage angle.

"Well, what do you think? Will we get permission?" he said when he had finished.

Mr. Martin rubbed his head again.

"Did you bang your head too?" he asked.

George tried to look offended.

"What's the angle?" said Mr. Martin.

"Angle?" said George. "There's no angle. It's our future that's at sake, you know. It might be tough on you having no books to teach with, but it's worse for us. You're dealing here with a generation that's going to grow up uneducated."

"I know," said Mr. Martin. "Believe me, I know. And you think books are going to make a difference?"

"Well, that's the idea, isn't it?" said George. "That's what you're all talking about all the time."

Mr. Martin locked the cabinet.

"Okay. Okay. I'll get the headmaster to see you after morning break. Be there, but I still want to know what the angle is."

Morning break wasn't too pleasant for George.

"Why did you have to go and tell him?" said Stick.

George explained patiently. "Because, dope, we'll need permission. You can't just go collecting money for something without permission. It's the way charities work. People get suspicious otherwise."

"Martin's suspicious already," said Tub.

"Only normally suspicious," said George. "Only the way teachers always are. It's part of their training. He doesn't know—"

"Know what?" said Sharon as George broke off.

"Nothing," he said. "I just meant he doesn't know us well enough to realize how concerned we are."

She looked doubtful. "I know you well enough," she said, "and I'm surprised. Not suspicious exactly, but surprised." George looked at her. Even the school uniform looked okay on Sharon.

"I've changed," he said. "I'm a better person now."

"Crawler," said Julia, and kicked him on the ankle.

Kev came out of a dream. "Sharon, you're brainy. What does percentage mean?"

Everybody began talking at once and Stick dug Kev in the ribs. Stick had sharp elbows. It was lucky Sharon never noticed Kev.

"Tell you what, George. I'll come with you to see the headmaster. I'll have to go to history first and explain, of course," she said.

"Oh, sure. Thanks, Sharon," said George.

She smiled at him. That made three times.

It was a strange feeling to be standing outside the headmaster's door knowing you hadn't done anything wrong—yet. He knocked and went in. Mr. Martin was already there. He seemed to be talking to the head about the school trip to France.

"I've just been explaining your idea, George," he said as George shut the door behind him.

The headmaster looked at George across his desk.

He was pretty normal for a headmaster. Careworn, a bit ragged around the edges. He looked as if he expected to be hit in the eye with a custard pie any minute.

"Aitken," he said. "I don't quite understand your wanting to do this. You're not in the school choir, are you?"

George sighed. There was a knock on the door and Sharon drifted through in shades of blond.

"Excuse me, Mr. Redfeather," she said. "I promised George I would come and help him explain."

The headmaster relaxed.

"Oh, you're involved in this, are you, Sharon?"

Sharon was in the school choir.

From then on it was a breeze. Ditto machine, school auditorium—it was theirs for the asking. The only fly in the ointment was that the head had put Mr. Martin in overall charge. Not that Mr. Martin had volunteered. In fact, when George remembered what Mr. Martin had been saying when he came in, he was certain that some kind of deal had been made. He was sure he had heard something about Mr. Martin's not having to take the school trip to France if he took this on.

Funny way to take your percentage, thought George. Shocking how every man had his price.

Once outside the headmaster's office, Sharon thanked Mr. Martin prettily and said she must be

36

going to history now. Mr. Martin leaned on the wall, hands in pockets. He looked kind of dog-eared.

"That's what tipped the balance," he said, nodding in Sharon's direction as she disappeared around the corner.

"I can't sing," said George before he could mention the school choir again.

"Not the point," said Mr. Martin.

He unfolded himself and began to walk along the corridor with George.

"Not in a hurry to get back to your class?"

"It's only English. I can speak English," said George.

"See what I mean. It's the attitude, George, the attitude."

"What's wrong with wanting to raise money for the school?" George said.

"Nothing at all," said Mr. Martin. "It's just that I can't help feeling that I'm missing something."

"What kind of thing?" said George.

"The angle," said Mr. Martin. "It's just not like you."

"Maybe I've changed," said George.

Mr. Martin stopped and looked at him.

"It's a possibility," he said. "Must be the love of a good woman."

George blushed. Mr. Martin laughed not unkindly. "Bring me your plan of attack by Friday lunchtime," he said, "and I'll go over it with you."

All through English George fumed. Talk about blackening a person's character. It was enough to make him do the thing for real just to show them. Forget about the percentage. He caught himself, sickened. See what they had driven him to? He mustn't let ideas like that take hold of him.

"Are you all right, Aitken?" asked Mr. Bell, the English teacher. "You seem to be muttering to yourself."

"Sorry, sir," said George. "I don't think I'm myself."

Mr. Bell smiled pleasantly.

"Well, don't think we're not grateful for that," he said. Mr. Bell was the sarcastic type.

They all met by the fountain again that evening. George arrived without Sharon. He knew it had been a great honor to hear her practice her cello, but his ears were sore. Maybe she hadn't played it for a while. She had seemed a bit upset when she let him in. All he'd said was there was a terrible noise coming from her living room and did she have a cat. What bothered him now, apart from the buzzing in his ears, was how to tell the rest what she had—no, they had—no, she had decided.

Stick was there already—dogless. That was a plus.

Julia was with him, which kind of canceled out the dog.

"No walkies tonight?" said George.

"It won't come out," said Stick morosely. "It's got agoraphobia."

"That's not what Mom said when she saw the lump on its head," said Julia.

Stick winced as if the memory were painful. "She took it to the vet," he said. "It's got a black eye."

"Oh, give it a rest, Stick," said George. "It's a black dog. Who's going to notice?"

"Where's Sharon?" said Julia. "I thought you were going to help her practice her cello. Did she stand you up?"

George gave her a look. "She's still practicing her cello," he said. "I left to come and meet you."

"She threw you out," said Julia.

"She did not throw me out. We agreed I should go." You had to be firm with Julia. Give her an inch and she took a mile.

"She threw you out," said Julia again.

"Only because I didn't recognize the tune she was playing," said George.

Stick wavered for a moment as if he still couldn't get it into his head that George wasn't responsible for the state of the dog. The habit of a lifetime was too strong. He came down on George's side.

"That's lousy. I mean, if you've never heard a tune before, how can you recognize it?"

Julia was not the type to give up. "What was the tune?" she said.

"The National Anthem," said George.

Tub and Kev arrived together. George was glad to see that Kev hadn't lost any more pieces of his anatomy. He decided to plunge straight into business and ignore Julia, who was singing "God Save the Queen."

"We've got to get a list of activities to show Martin on Friday," he said. "Any suggestions?"

"We could have a sponsored walk," said Stick.

"Boring," said Julia. At least it stopped her singing.

"I don't like walking," said Tub. "Why is she singing the National Anthem?"

"Nobody's asking you to like it," said George.

"Like it?" said Tub. "It sounds like a cat with the heebie-jeebies."

George didn't want to hear about cats. He also had the feeling he was losing his grip on this meeting.

"Forget Julia. She's stopped now anyway. I meant nobody's asking you to like walking. Just think of the percentage."

Tub and Kev spoke together.

Tub said, "Forget Julia—some hope."

Kev said, "What's a percentage?"

Julia barged into Tub and squared up to Kev, all in one fluid movement. Her eyes were about level with the logo on his sweatshirt.

"Look, Kev," she said, prodding him. "The percentage is what we get out of it. Think of it as a fee, the rakeoff, our cut."

Kev brightened up. "I don't mind walking," he said.

Tub looked unconvinced.

"Okay," said Stick, "what do you like doing?"

"Snorkeling," said Tub.

George weighed the odds. He was going to need all the help he could get if he wanted to put Sharon's idea across after that business with the National Anthem. "Okay, we'll have a sponsored snorkel. It's different. What else?"

"A rummage sale," said Julia.

"Now look who's being boring," said George.

"It might be boring," said Julia, "but it's profitable. It's a well-known fact that you make more money out of rummage sales than any other kind of fundraising."

"Says who?" said Stick.

"Says Mom," said Julia. "*And* she says she's got a lot of junk she wants to get rid of."

"Sounds like a good idea," Stick said.

"Chicken," said Tub.

"You didn't hear what she said about the dog," he said.

"Okay," said George. "That's a sponsored snorkel and a rummage sale."

"Besides," said Julia, "we might find something

valuable. People are always finding things worth thousands of pounds at rummage sales."

Tub chimed in, "That's right. My mom always watches *Antiques Roadshow*, and just about everything comes out of attics and rummage sales and things."

Tub's mother watched the funniest programs.

"Anything else?" said George.

"We could bag groceries at the supermarket," said Kev. "It's always crawling with scouts and things doing that." They all looked at him. Nobody had expected Kev to have an idea.

"Great," said George before anybody else had recovered. Now was the moment while they were still in shock from Kev's making a suggestion. "Sharon had an idea," he said, moving casually to the other side of the pond. He aimed a stone or two at the cherub for luck. Better to put as much distance between himself and the rest as possible. He might have to fight his way out. "She thinks we should have a concert."

It took a moment for this to penetrate, then they all spoke at once.

"I'm not going anywhere near a stage," said Tub.

"You mean singing and dancing and that? No way," said Stick.

"Mom will make me do my rotten ballet," said Julia.

"I could play the drums," Kev said.

"I didn't know you played the drums," said Tub.

"I don't but I could."

"What do you mean, you could?" said Stick.

Kev looked puzzled. "It's easy," he said. "You just hit them. I'm good at hitting things."

"A concert, then," said George quickly. "And we don't have to worry about organizing it. Sharon's going to do that. I'll make a list of suggestions and give it to Mr. Martin on Friday."

It hadn't been as bad as he had thought, thanks to Kev. He felt quite kindly toward Kev.

"How's the gnome?" he said.

"It got a bit chipped when the back of the trailer blew off," said Kev.

"Well, that's progress," said George.

"Oh, it's not much," said Kev modestly. "It gave me an idea though."

"What, another one? You want to watch out for that, Kev," said Tub.

"Shut up, Tub," said Stick. He found himself strangely drawn to the saga of the battle between Kev and the gnome.

"I thought I would try a pickax," said Kev.

"Have you got a pickax?" said Julia, impressed.

"No, but I know where I can get one."

"That's handy," said George. "I suppose it'll be practice for the drums."

His mind was on other things. Like working out how to fix the percentage. With Mr. Martin in charge, it wouldn't be easy. And then there was Sharon. It had all seemed so simple when he first thought of it. Then he thought about the skateboard. It was worth it.

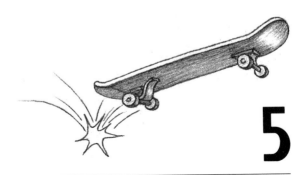

5

One good thing about the project was that the group was excused from afternoon classes on Friday to prepare the publicity material. Mr. Martin had approved the list and given them a list in return. It was a lot longer than theirs had been. They all gathered in the resource center after lunch.

"I never thought there would be this much to do," said Tub.

"We have to be organized," said Sharon. "Now, Philip, you can get started on the posters while I do the stencils for the Ditto machine."

They all looked around—even Mr. Martin. Nobody had come in.

"Who's Philip?" said George.

Sharon looked meaningfully at Tub. He was still looking around to see who had come in. He stopped.

"Oh, sorry. It's me. I forgot."

"I didn't know you were called Philip," said Julia.

"I'm not," said Tub. "I'm called Tub. I've always been called Tub, but Philip's my name."

"Why don't you call him Tub. Everybody else does. Even the teachers," said Stick to Sharon.

Mr. Martin nodded in agreement.

"Nicknames are demeaning," said Sharon. "Don't you think so, Mr. Martin."

"What's demeaning?" said Kev.

"Nicknames, cloth ears," said Tub.

"Well, Sharon, sometimes they can be a sign of friendship," said Mr. Martin.

"No, I mean, what's the meaning of demeaning?" said Kev.

"I can't work out the question," said Stick.

"Look, Kev," said Mr. Martin, "if I called you Godzilla, that would be demeaning."

"People call me that all the time," said Kev.

George smiled. It was nice to see someone else on the receiving end for a change. He tried to think of something really demeaning to call Kev. It was impossible. He looked at Mr. Martin's list instead.

"Posters, leaflets, concert tickets, collecting-can labels, sponsor-sheet forms," he said. "We'll be here all night."

"Not if you let Sharon organize you," said Mr. Martin. "I'll be in the office if you need me."

"Trust a teacher to avoid all the work," said Julia when he'd gone.

"You can work the Ditto machine, Julia," said Sharon. "I've finished the design for the leaflet. You run it off while I do the sponsor sheets."

"Thanks a million," said Julia.

After several false starts she managed to get the sheet in the right way. There seemed to be a good deal of purple ink all over her.

"Why don't we have a photocopier like normal schools?" she said.

"We do," said Sharon, "but the Ditto's cheaper. Now, George, you make a start on the concert tickets. Paul, you can help George."

"What can I do?" said Kev.

"Good question," said Tub.

Sharon looked doubtful.

"I suppose you could take over the Ditto machine and let Julia get started on the labels for the collecting cans."

"Good," said Julia. "My arm's sore already."

Kev took over willingly. Nobody complained when sheets started to fly out of the machine like bullets. He had to do something.

By the time they had finished, Julia had managed to smear the purple ink from her face into her hair.

Kev's arm was hanging limply by his side. Tub's knees were sore from crawling around the floor doing posters, and Stick had nearly sliced off three of George's fingers with the paper cutter while he was helping him cut up the tickets. Sharon looked terrific, as usual.

Mr. Martin poked his head around the door. He was looking nervous.

"Mr. Hughes is outside," he said. "He wants to lock up."

Mr. Hughes was the janitor.

"Just finished," said George. "We'd better get out. Everybody take a bundle of stuff." Everybody did. Opinions differed about who ran the school, Mr. Redfeather or Mr. Hughes, but most people would have voted for the janitor. He stood outside as they passed him, jangling his keys and counting them as they came out. He was always counting them. Nobody knew why.

"Kids," he said to Mr. Martin. "Nothing but trouble."

Mr. Martin smiled. "Anybody would think the school was run for their benefit," he said.

The janitor nodded and began locking up. The group trundled off down the corridor.

"Wasted on him," said George to Mr. Martin sympathetically.

"How do you know I wasn't serious?" said Mr. Martin.

George grinned. He liked Mr. Martin. It was a pity they couldn't let him in for a cut of the profits, but that would be going too far. Besides, he was getting out of having to take the school trip.

"I've phoned the supermarket manager," said Mr. Martin. "He has agreed to let you pack tomorrow morning. I've also got some students from the lower grades lined up to lend a hand."

"Kids?" said George. "We don't want little kids."

"Take what you can get, George," said Mr. Martin. "They were the only ones I could force into it."

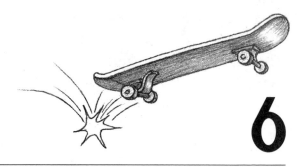

6

Looking back, packing at the supermarket was a breeze compared with the rest of the week. None of George's friends thought so at the time. After all, when you read things in the paper like NEAR RIOT AT LOCAL SUPERMARKET, you don't rate it as a success. Nevertheless, they were to look back on the supermarket fiasco as an oasis of calm, a practice for the real disasters. George met Stick on the way to the market. They walked across the parking lot together. George was thinking about the skateboard—as usual. There was a long, sloping ramp up to the main doors of the supermarket. George was imagining himself skimming down it on the skateboard. It would be great.

"My mom says she's coming to do her shopping here this morning, and she wants it packed free," said Stick.

George shook his head. "I hope you told her that was corruption."

Stick gave him a look. "You must be joking."

They walked up the ramp toward the store, past rows and rows of shopping carts. George looked at them in awe.

"Are we going to have to pack all those?"

Half a dozen younger kids had turned up looking depressingly eager. Sharon handed out sticky labels which she referred to as their official collectors' badges. She stationed them each at a checkout. She also said she would be acting in a supervisory capacity.

Tub snorted. "That means she won't be doing any work. Why can't she just say so instead of showing off how many big words she knows?"

"What's the charge?" asked Amanda, one of the younger kids.

"There's no charge," said Sharon. "People will make a donation."

"Some hope," said Julia.

"And you must not rattle the collecting can under their noses," said Sharon. "I'm putting them at the end of the checkout counters so that people will be free to make whatever contribution they want."

"How are we going to make money that way?" said Stick. "Why don't we just charge them fifty pence each?"

"It's a charity, Paul," said Sharon. "You've got to allow them to give what they can. After all, you can't charge a senior citizen the same as everybody else."

Amanda looked at Stick as if he'd just mugged her grandmother.

"Now, if anyone wants groceries wheeled out to the parking lot, you have to catch my attention," said Sharon. "I'll get one of you who isn't too busy to do it. We have to finish at twelve. Okay. Any questions?"

"Only what did your last slave die of," said Julia under her breath.

Business was a bit slow to start, but once it built up, George began to see a problem. By the time he had finished the packing, the shopper had paid the cashier and dropped some money in the can. Nobody but nobody handed him their money. He looked around at the others. It seemed to be the same with them. So if the money all went straight into the cans, how was the percentage to be made? He didn't have a customer, so he allowed his mind to mull the problem over.

He looked around the store. Outside the big glass walls he could see several people with collecting cans. It seemed to be some kind of flag day. Inside he counted two lottery booths, a kitchen competition, and several slot machines. Talk about a pay-as-you-enter supermarket. Shopping seemed to be a minor activity as far as he could see. Everybody's got something going, he thought. Then the solution hit him. All he had to do was hide one of the cans at the end. Simple. Well, simple so long as Sharon was out of the way. He might have to create a diversion.

It was an hour or so before George noticed a steady trickle of people coming back to complain. Several of them were demanding in loud voices to see the manager, and a small group of angry-looking women had gathered around Kev's checkout.

"Look," said one. "See what he's doing. No wonder my eggs got broken."

"Cookies at the bottom with all the cans piled on top," said another. "It's a disgrace. If they can't do it right, they shouldn't be allowed to do it at all."

"I want the money I put in that can back," said another, "and a new box of cornflakes."

The woman Kev was packing for was surrounded by the knot of women. Kev was continuing anyway. George had a look at his technique. It was simple but effective. He just shoved the stuff into a carton as it came off the conveyor belt, and if it wouldn't fit, he hammered it down till it did. It didn't do the groceries a lot of good, but at least it got everything in.

Sharon appeared just as the manager arrived, looking like thunder. George couldn't hear what she was saying to him, but the melting look was having its effect. He was getting visibly calmer.

With a strength he would not have thought her capable of, she reached out a hand and yanked Kev away from the groceries he was reducing to pulp. It must be her bowing arm, thought George. He hadn't realized playing the cello developed the muscles.

"George," she said as she passed him, dragging Kev behind her, "I'm putting Kev outside." She made him sound like the trash, which was probably the way she thought of him anyway. "If there are any carts to be wheeled to the parking lot, he'll do it," she went on.

"Okay, Sharon," said George. "Anything you say." He barely kept himself from saluting.

Things got gradually quieter as the trail of Kev's customers finally dried up. By that time the manager was handing out free groceries to anybody who as much as said good morning. At a quarter to twelve George decided it was time for action on the percentage front. Sharon was patrolling the checkouts like a prison guard, and the assistants were keeping wary eyes on the packers. The only one who was not being watched was Kev. George would have preferred one of the others, but there was nothing else to do.

Kev had just wheeled a loaded cart out onto the ramp beyond the glass wall. George waited until Sharon's back was turned and began to wave to catch his attention. Kev waved back and grinned. George ground his teeth. If he was quick, Sharon would never notice he had gone. He sneaked across to the window.

"Create a diversion," he mouthed to Kev.

"What?" bellowed Kev.

George waved his hands. "Shut up," he mouthed. His breath was steaming up the window on the inside. Kev tried to wipe it clear on the outside and looked puzzled when nothing happened. George moved a little and put both hands around his mouth. "Create a diversion," he mouthed against the glass.

Kev put both hands up to his own mouth. "What?" he yelled.

George saw it coming. For a moment he stood rooted to the spot, staring at Kev's cart. It could have been happening in slow motion. George lunged forward to stop it and banged his nose on the glass. It began to bleed. He didn't notice. He was watching in silent fascination as the cart Kev had been holding on to before he put both hands to his mouth rolled slowly down the ramp. Kev was banging on the glass, trying to attract his attention. The supermarket had not been open long, so the carts were still in good condition, none of this rusty-wheel-jamming stuff.

Halfway down the ramp the cart was picking up speed nicely and making straight for a row of empty carts.

If it had been planned, it wouldn't have happened. It fit itself neatly into the first empty cart. There was a moment's pause before the long, long line began to move. Kev's cart had been heavily loaded, and it was no time at all before it picked up speed again, adding a few more carts along the way. All in all, there must have been about twenty of them all neatly fitted together. They made a low, rumbling noise as they gathered speed down the ramp.

By this time other people were beginning to realize that there was some kind of free entertainment going on outside. Gradually the window filled up with silent watchers, the cash registers stopped buzzing, the flag sellers fell silent. Even the slot machines grew quiet as the crowd craned their necks to see what was happening. The snakelike line of carts traveled on toward the bottom of the ramp, going at a fast lick now and glinting prettily in the sunshine. It was heading straight for one of the short concrete posts that divided the parking lot from the area in front of the market.

There was a crash as the front cart came in contact with the post, and the line split asunder like a shining cluster of asteroids. After that it was the noise that caught everybody's attention. Car brakes squealing, horns honking, the crunch of metal on metal. George could have stayed and watched, but he remembered something more important. He slipped out of the crowd and hid the collecting can from the nearest cash register under an upside-down carton. He had the feeling his group would not be staying long. For the first time he noticed he was covered in blood. He was puzzled for a moment before his nose began to hurt. After it was all over, certain pictures stayed in George's memory—like the store manager standing there pale and trembling, saying, "They should never have built that parking lot at the bottom of a slope. I can't understand what they were thinking of."

"The trees," said Kev.

"What?" said the manager.

"Nothing," said George. "Ignore him."

The manager yelled at him. "I don't know how, but this is your fault and if you ever set foot in this store again, I'll call the police."

And, worse than that, the kid called Amanda was saying, "Oh, look what I've found under this carton. It must have fallen over." She handed the collecting can he had hidden—their percentage—to Sharon.

Sharon didn't say a word on the way home, and nobody complained when she stalked on ahead.

As it happened, Kev was the first to speak. "What were you saying to me through the window, George?"

"Create a diversion," said George.

"What's a diversion?" said Kev.

Nobody answered.

When George got home, his mother said, "What happened to your nose?"

"I walked into a plate glass window," said George.

"Dreaming again, George," she said as she hauled him off to the bathroom. "One of these days you'll walk into real trouble."

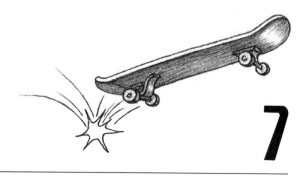

7

Nobody was surprised when Mr. Martin met George and his friends coming out of assembly on Monday morning and told them the headmaster wanted to see them. They filed into Mr. Redfeather's office silently and stood in front of his desk. They jostled a bit, each of them trying to get to the back. It had to stop when they finally wedged themselves back against the door in a clump. There were only the six of them—George, Stick, Sharon, Julia, Kev, and Tub. The younger kids had not been made to come, which George supposed was fair enough. He didn't mind that, but he would have liked to see Amanda get it in the neck.

The head stared at them sadly. He was looking as if somebody had hit him in the eye with that custard pie at last. He did a quick double-take when he saw Kev. George didn't blame him. Kev's eyebrows had started sprouting again—not everywhere, just the odd tuft here and there.

"The supermarket manager has been in touch with me," said Mr. Redfeather. "He didn't have a great deal of time to spare since he was getting ready to leave."

"Where's he going?" asked Tub, brightening a little.

"He tells me he is being transferred to Wick," said the headmaster.

"Where's Wick?" said Stick.

"He was asking me that too," said the headmaster. "It's in the north of Scotland, the very north of Scotland. However, he did have time to give me a brief outline of the events of Saturday morning and, although he cannot be certain of what actually happened, he is convinced that you were at the root of it."

They all tried to take a step back, which was impossible since they were already as far back as they could go.

"Can any of you give me an explanation?"

Silence.

He sighed and pushed a newspaper across the desk at them. "Perhaps you would like to take a look at this," he said. "It says: 'Near Riot at Local Supermarket.' Just under the article on the museum theft."

They clustered around as George picked up the paper.

"There can't have been that many cars damaged," said Julia. "The papers are always exaggerating. Just wait till I see that reporter again."

A horrible suspicion flowered in George's mind. "What do you mean, again?" he said. "You mean you got in touch with the papers?"

"Well, you said I was in charge of publicity," said Julia. "How did I know there was going to be a riot?"

"Good publicity," said George. "You're the one that wants to be a reporter. This is what's called getting bad press."

"He doesn't say it had anything to do with us," said Julia. "He just says at the end that we were collecting for a school book fund."

The headmaster interrupted.

"I'm afraid for once I have to agree with Aitken," he said. "He doesn't actually say you were involved, but tacking it on to the end of the story like that does produce a certain impression. It's the implication, Julia."

Sharon took over. "I'm afraid we are rather confused ourselves over what happened, Mr. Redfeather. Philip, Paul, Julia, and I were all busy at the time repacking some boxes that had been brought back."

She shot a look at Kev. If looks could kill, he would have been dead and buried. Kev didn't notice.

"Philip? Who's Philip?" the headmaster said.

"Me," said Tub.

"Oh, yes, so it is," said the head. Then he looked at George. "And you, George. Do you have anything to say?"

George smelled trouble. Calling the boys by their first names was always a bad sign with the head-master.

"It did seem a bit crazy to have the carts all lined up on the ramp like that," he said, trying to sidestep the question. "I mean, the slightest thing could have done it."

"Yeah," said Kev helpfully. "I mean, I only took my hands off the—"

George kicked him hard, but fortunately the head never took any notice of Kev—not since Kev fell through his study window while practicing abseiling from the school roof. That was a couple of years ago, before he got interested in plants and things, when he still thought he wanted to go into the army when he left school.

"Yes, yes," said the head. "It seems they are going to change that now, but I understand the company will have to pay out a good deal of money in compensation. I would like to think you had nothing to do with it, George."

George would like him to think that too.

"I was behind a plate glass window when it happened, sir," he said.

He could see the head trying to decide whether to go on with it or let it go. Discretion won.

"All right," he said, "I will accept your word, but if there's any more trouble connected with this project, any at all, I will insist on its being dropped, books or no books. You may go."

They didn't need telling twice.

"Not bad, George," said Tub.

"Why did you kick me?" said Kev.

"I have never been called up in front of the headmaster like that before," said Sharon.

"Where is Wick exactly?" said Stick.

"Do you think he believed us?" said Julia.

"What did you say to that reporter?" said George.

They bickered their way down the corridor and George was in the classroom before he realized he still had the head's newspaper. He stuffed it in his pocket. He wasn't going back into Mr. Redfeather's office if he could help it.

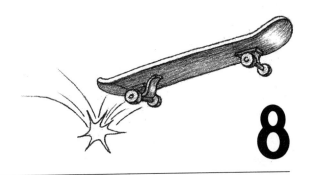

8

Apart from the interview with the head, the week started quietly enough. Mr. Martin had been busy arranging events. The sponsored snorkel would be on Friday evening, the rummage sale on Saturday afternoon, and the concert on Saturday evening, both in the school auditorium. George suspected him of trying to get it over with in a lump and said so.

"Nothing of the kind, George," he said. "It suits the janitor to have both on the same day. He's going to take a self-defense course the next weekend."

George couldn't tell if he was joking.

Sponsor forms and leaflets telling people not to bring rummage to the auditorium until after school on Friday were handed out to all the classes. George called a meeting at the fountain for Tuesday evening. They didn't tell Sharon. She was busy organizing the concert and practicing her cello. She was playing a solo. George hoped it would be the National Anthem so that he would recognize it this time. With one thing and another, he figured he had lost a lot of ground with Sharon. Maybe it was the way she had looked at him when she told him that her unblemished record at school was now broken and she held him personally responsible. He wished she wouldn't talk like that.

"It was Kev that let go of the cart," George had said. She had given him one of those looks—the kind that made him feel about three years old.

"Am I my brother's keeper?" she said. Sharon had won the religious knowledge prize three years in a row.

George didn't say anything. He thought keeper was just about right when it came to Kev.

Julia was in a rotten mood.

"I told you," she said. "I knew it would happen. Mom wants me to do my ballet at the lousy concert."

"You think that's bad," said Stick. He wasn't feeling too great anyway because he'd had to bring the dog. It dragged along at the end of its leash, choking itself. "Sharon's put me in the choir. She says they need baritones." His voice was a deep growl.

"What's a baritone?" said Kev.

"I don't know," said Stick. "She just said they needed baritones and put me in the back row."

"She must mean tall people," said Tub, shifting something around inside his mouth. Whatever it was rattled horribly against his teeth.

"What are you eating?" said Julia.

"Fizz bullets," he said. "Want one?"

He held out a paper bag to Julia. She tried to pick one up, but they all stuck together in a lump.

"Sorry," said Tub. "I was sitting on a radiator at lunchtime and they were in my pocket."

He broke the lump and offered one of the candies to Julia. Several scattered on the ground.

"No thanks," said Julia, looking at the sticky mess. "I've changed my mind."

"You'll rot your teeth," said George.

"They're not as bad as toffees," said Tub. "Toffees are definitely worse."

"You're the expert," said George. He threw a stone moodily at the cherub and missed. He didn't often miss.

"What's wrong with you?" said Stick.

"What do you think?" said George. His nose was still hurting. "All that work on Friday printing posters and leaflets. Then getting our heads bitten off by that supermarket guy. Then the head yesterday. And we haven't even made a penny from it."

It took a lot to get George down, so they did their best to cheer him up, all except Julia.

"That guy's gone to Wick," said Stick, "wherever that is."

"The head never bothers us if we don't bother him," said Tub.

"We'll make money out of the snorkel," said Kev.

"You're just annoyed because Sharon's mad at you again," said Julia.

George ignored her. He turned to Kev.

"How do we make money out of the snorkel?" he said, but Kev was looking at the dog.

"Has your dog got rabies?" he said to Stick.

"No, agoraphobia," said Stick. "You're thinking of hydrophobia."

"No, I'm not," said Kev. "I've never heard of hydro—whatever it is."

"It's got a black eye," said Julia.

"I thought it was rabies when they foamed at the mouth," said Kev.

Stick looked at the dog and turned pale. Sure enough, pink foam was bubbling out of the sides of its mouth.

"She'll kill me if it's got rabies," he said. "How could it get rabies?"

"It has to be bitten by something mad," said Kev.

They all looked at him. Nobody could actually believe he had bitten the dog. Still . . .

Then Tub spoke. "It's okay," he said. "It's the fizz bullets."

"What, those candies?" said Stick.

"Yeah, they fizz up when you bite them."

They all looked at the dog. Pink foam was still dribbling out of its mouth and it was hunting around for another candy. It seemed to have perked up a bit.

"Forget the dog," said George. "How are we going to make money out of the snorkel?"

They all thought.

"We could forge some names on the sponsor sheets," said Tub.

"Then we'd have to fork out more money," said George. "It's fewer names than you've got sponsoring you that we need, not more."

Tub thought for a minute.

"Oh, yeah, you're right," he said.

"We could hand in only some of the money," said Stick. "Say people were out when we called to collect it."

"They sign when they pay," said George.

They thought again.

"I've got it," said Julia, "we just forge some extra sheets."

"No good," said George. "The sheets all have to be numbered and stamped with the school stamp. I tell you, it's hopeless."

"Okay, we forget about making money out of the snorkel," said Stick. "There's still the rummage sale and the concert."

"And we do the snorkel for real?" said George.

"Cheer up, George," said Tub. "How about threatening people with a rabid dog unless they give us money?"

At that the dog belched loudly and more pink foam bubbled up through its teeth. It seemed to be grinning.

"Glad somebody's happy anyway," said George. It was hard to let go of the idea of making the percentage on the snorkel.

"Right," he said, "rummage collection every night this week and we'll take the sponsor forms with us. We don't have to be too bothered about getting names, but we have to make it look as if we're trying."

"Where are we going to keep the rummage?" asked Tub. "Old Hughes won't let it in the school before next Friday."

"We'll just have to keep it at home," said George, "unless anybody has a better idea."

"We could have kept it in our trailer," said Kev, "if we still had a trailer."

"We could have kept it in the hut down by the common," said Stick, "if there was still a hut down by the common."

"No, you couldn't," said Kev. He wasn't in the least

offended. "That belonged to the cubs. Tell you what though. There's a big old house around our way they're going to demolish. We could find somewhere there to keep it."

"Waste of money," said Tub, rattling another fizz bullet around his teeth.

"What is?" said George.

"Employing people to demolish a house around Kev's way," he said. "All they have to do is let him loose in it for a couple of hours."

It was decided that they would keep the stuff in the old house.

"That's fine," said Kev. "I've been meaning to go there anyway."

"What for?" said Stick.

"A pickax," said Kev.

"Ask a stupid question," said Stick.

The gnome was in everyone's thoughts.

"You really hate that gnome, don't you, Kev?" said George.

"If it wasn't for that gnome, Mom wouldn't want a patio," said Kev. "And besides, it's horrible, really horrible. It looks evil."

"It must be bad," said Julia.

The rest nodded. If Kev thought the gnome looked evil, it must be really horrible.

"All right," said Stick, "we'll meet at this house tomorrow, then, and bring whatever rummage we've got. What time?"

"Eight? Eight-thirty?" said Tub.

"Eight," said Stick. "Okay, everybody?"

George didn't say anything.

"Okay, George?" said Stick.

"I might be a bit late," said George. "I've got to go to Sharon's at eight to rehearse."

"Rehearse what?"

"Oh, just a thing," said George.

"What kind of thing?" said Stick.

They were all interested by this time.

"A play kind of thing."

They had all the patience in the world. They'd got a whiff of something good coming.

"What kind of play thing?" said Tub.

"A Shakespeare thing."

"What, you mean like that thing we did about the fairies and the wall and the guy called Bottom?" said Tub.

"No, something else," said George.

"Hamlet," said Stick. "Alas poor Kciroy, I knew him backward."

George shook his head.

"What then?"

There was no way they were going to let it go.

"Look, it's nothing," said George. "She just stands on this balcony thing and I talk at her."

"Doesn't sound very exciting," said Tub. "No sword fights?"

"It's *Romeo and Juliet*," yelled Julia, dancing

around George. "You're doing the balcony scene with Sharon. Barf."

George threw another stone at the cherub. It rocked on its pedestal.

"It's all right for you," he shouted. "How do you think I'm going to feel?"

"Oh, Romeo, Romeo," said Julia, clutching her T-shirt.

George stomped off.

"You can't play Romeo with a nose like that," Stick shouted after him.

"She'll make you wear tights," yelled Julia.

George continued to stomp.

"Who's this guy Romeo anyway?" said Kev.

"Romeo?" said Tub. "He's worse than your gnome."

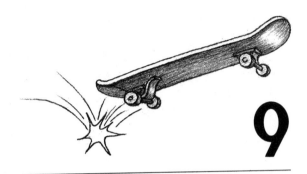

9

Things didn't get much better for George on Wednesday. It was bad enough having to rehearse the balcony thing, but Sharon had gotten him a costume as well. She must have been collecting rummage too. He looked in disgust at the things. There was a dark green velvet vest and a frilly blouse with big sleeves.

"I won't show you my costume. I'm keeping it as a surprise," said Sharon. "All you'll need is a pair of tights and it'll be perfect, George."

"With this stuff, all I need is a Gypsy violin," said George. Then he realized what she'd said. He looked at her in horror. His voice came out in a strangulated gulp. "Tights?"

"Now, George, don't be silly about this. You've got to look the part."

"I'm already going to look like something that's escaped from *The Sound of Music*. I'm not wearing tights," said George. "I'd never live it down."

The thought of Julia rose up before his eyes, and he shuddered.

"No tights," he said again.

"You've got to," said Sharon.

George lost count of the number of times he said "no tights" till Sharon got in a huff and threw him out again.

"We'll see," she said darkly as he slouched off down the path.

George's mind was made up, and not even Sharon Taylor was going to change it. She might look like a shampoo ad, but he wondered if there wasn't a flaw in her character. There were things you just did not ask a man to do, and wearing tights was at the top of the list. He made his way to the fountain, but there was nobody there.

"Tights," he said to the cherub, and got it in the eye with a pebble.

He walked on through the bottom gate of the park toward the old house on the far side of the common. On the way he passed the moldering remains of the cub hut.

"Good work, Kev," he muttered as he passed.

The house looked as if it wouldn't take much to demolish it. Windows were broken and the roof had caved in at a couple of places. Even the danger sign had fallen down. He heard the rest before he saw them. They seemed to be arguing. They were in the front hall. The door screeched as he pushed his way through, but nobody noticed. They were all talking at once. The hall was so big, the sound echoed and bounced off the walls. He stood there for a moment, watching them.

Kev was kicking bits of plaster out of the wall with his size elevens. Tub was trying to talk through a mouthful of toffee. Stick was perched on the banisters, which didn't look too safe, his long legs dangling. He was shouting at Julia. Julia was standing in the middle of them all with an ugly green vase in her hand. She was shouting at everybody. It was anybody's guess whom she was thinking of throwing the vase at. Oh, well, thought George, they might have their faults, but they wouldn't ask him to wear tights.

"What's up?" he said.

Julia turned to him.

"It's these idiots," she said. "They're totally ignorant. I don't know why they bother going to school. It's not as if they've ever learned anything."

George looked at them.

"So what else is new?" he said. "They've been ignorant for years. They're good at it. If you could get an A in ignorance, they'd be sure things."

"Have you ever heard of Ming?" she said.

George thought.

"I don't suppose it's the guy that's got the Chinese takeout on Bellarmine Street," he said.

"Stop trying to be funny," she yelled. "Ming. Ming. Ming."

"Hello, who's there?" said Stick, and fell off the banister laughing.

George made the connection. Art history—Ming dynasty—priceless porcelain—china from China, in fact. Who said education was wasted?

He looked at the vase. It was an ugly-looking thing, but it looked old. Not that old though—not Ming dynasty. That was the kind of stuff they kept in museums.

He shook his head.

"It can't be," he said. "Things like that just don't happen. At least, not to us."

"It is," said Julia.

George thought of Tub's mother and the *Antiques Roadshow*.

"How do you know?" he said.

"Because it says so on the bottom," said Julia. "Look." She turned the vase over and there on the bottom, surrounded by a lot of Chinese symbols, was the word "Ming."

Tub had finished his toffee.

"What's the panic?" he said.

"It's nothing," said Julia sarcastically. "Only that we've got a vase worth hundreds, no thousands, probably hundreds of thousands of pounds."

Stick poked his head through a gap in the stair rails and whistled.

"What, that old thing?"

Kev stopped kicking the wall.

"*How* much?"

Where did you get it?" said George.

"Here," said Julia.

"Here?" repeated George. "What, just lying around?"

"We were looking for a place to stash the rummage," said Tub, "and Julia found this big closet. There was all kinds of stuff lying around in it. I bet we won't have to do any more collecting. There's enough for two rummage sales there."

Julia shook her head sadly.

"He still doesn't understand. Look, dope," she said, turning on him, "we'll never have to collect anything else in our lives again. We're rich."

"I found the pickax," said Kev, starting to kick the wall again.

"Why are you wasting time with the boot, then?" said George, looking at the hole in the wall.

Julia was dancing around again. The vase slipped and George lunged. He caught it just before it hit the floor.

"Hey, that was good," said Tub. "Why can't you do that when you're playing goal?"

"Because the ball isn't worth thousands of pounds," said George through his teeth. "Julia, don't do that again."

"Sorry," said Julia.

That had more effect on them than anything. There was a short silence while it came home to the rest that something serious was going on. It had to be serious. Nobody could ever remember Julia saying sorry before.

"We'll take it to that antiques shop on High Street in the morning," said George.

"They'll ask us where we got it," said Julia.

"Well, we'll tell them," said George. "After all, nobody has lived in this house for years. It's not as if we've pinched it. It was just lying around."

"You don't suppose it *is* stolen," said Tub, "and the thieves have hidden it here."

"You've been reading comics again," said George. "You'll rot your brain as well as your teeth. Would you steal a Ming vase then just leave it lying around in a closet? Don't be an idiot."

"Who did, then?" said Stick. "Leave it lying around, I mean."

"Some ignoramus who didn't know anything about Ming," said Julia pointedly.

"Who's going to take charge of it?" said George. As if he didn't know.

"You," said Julia. "If I take it home, Stick'll probably sit on it."

"We'll need something to wrap it in," said George.

"What's that stuffed down your jacket?" said Kev.

George looked at his Romeo costume.

"Rummage," he said.

"Wrap it in that," said Julia.

George found the headmaster's newspaper in his pocket and stuffed the vase with it before wrapping it up in the costume. He wedged the whole thing inside his jacket and zipped it up.

"Don't come near me," he said. "I don't want any accidents."

They gave him a wide berth all the way home. George amused himself by hurling insults at them. He would never be safer.

"Nine o'clock outside the antiques shop," he said as he turned in at his house. It was touching the way they had all seen him safely to his door.

"We'll be in trouble for missing school," said Stick.

"It's worth it," said Julia.

George listened to them as they disappeared down the street.

"I forgot to bring the pickax," Kev was saying.

His mother was vacuuming the stair carpet when he got in. She didn't have time during the day, what with working and all.

"What's that stuffed down your jacket, George?" she said.

"Rummage," said George.

The vacuum cleaner gave a sort of whine and bits of soil burst out of the hose and scattered everywhere. There was a smell of burning rubber.

"You might as well take this for your rummage sale," she said when she saw his face. "Don't worry. The weeding was a great idea—the vacuum was on its last legs anyway." She looked tired.

George wanted to tell her that after tomorrow she could have a hundred vacuum cleaners, but he thought he would keep it as a surprise.

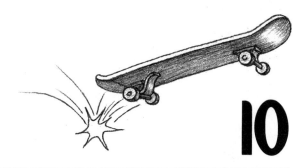

10

The group was at the antiques shop at nine sharp. All present and accounted for. Nobody wanted to miss this.

"Okay, then," George said. "Let me do the talking. Come on."

They all barged in the door at the same time.

"Get back," said George. "You don't want the thing broken at this stage."

They fell in behind him as he pushed open the door. There was an old man behind the counter wearing half glasses. He didn't look too happy to see them.

"Watch yourselves," he said. "There's valuable stuff in here."

He pointed at a notice on the wall. It was one of those revolting rhymes.

Lovely to look at
Delightful to hold
If you should break it
We consider it sold.

They stood there nervously. The shop was so crammed full of bits of furniture and china and glass, there was hardly room for all of them.

"We've brought you something really special," said George.

"And I've heard that one before," he said sourly. He wasn't exactly a ray of sunshine. "Okay, let's have a look at it," he went on. Then he added, "Careful," as they all crowded around the counter.

George lifted the vase still wrapped in his Romeo costume out of his bag and laid it carefully on the counter. He began to unwrap it.

"It really is special," he said. "Look." He removed the vase from the folds of the frilly blouse.

The man looked at it and picked it up, turning it around. He didn't say anything while he plunged his hand inside and took out the newspaper.

"Where did you get it?" he said at last.

George decided to tell the truth. He couldn't think of anything better offhand.

"Lying around in an old house that's going to be demolished."

"You didn't steal it?"

"Steal it?" said George. "No, we didn't steal it. I told you, it was lying around at the back of a closet in this old house."

The shopkeeper pursed his lips and examined the vase carefully. He turned it upside down and looked at the markings on the bottom. They held their breath.

"All right," he said at last. "I'll believe you, though thousands wouldn't."

He had a really original line.

"I'll give you fifteen pounds for it," he said.

They gasped.

"Fifteen," screeched Tub. "Fifteen?"

"Okay, then, seventeen," he said, "but that's my final offer. I don't say it's not a nice bit of china, but this stuff is going out of fashion now. There's a lot of it around."

George couldn't believe his ears.

"Well, it *would* be out of fashion, wouldn't it?" he said. "I mean, it's hundreds of years old—maybe thousands."

"Hundreds of years old?" the old man said. "Don't talk nonsense. It's no more than fifty years old."

"It's Ming," said Julia from somewhere behind Stick. Her furious face appeared under his armpit.

"It says so on the bottom."

The old guy nearly smiled.

"So it's Ming, is it? And what do you know about Ming?"

"Not a lot," Tub put in, "only that it's worth thousands of pounds."

The antiques dealer leaned across the counter.

"Well, let me tell you a thing or two about Ming. The Ming dynasty in China was somewhere around five hundred years ago, mainly during the fifteenth century, and there wasn't much green porcelain made. Mainly blue and white or maybe some red and a little yellow. And one thing more, they did not write the word 'Ming' in English on the bottom of vases."

His words hung in the air. It took a minute for them to sink in, and when they did, George wished the floor would open and swallow him up. It was so obvious. It was like the pyramids having Made in Egypt stamped across them. How could he have missed it?

"Not Ming?" said Tub.

"Not Ming," said the man.

"Seventeen pounds is quite a lot of money," said Kev.

George thought it was the most sensible thing he had ever heard Kev say.

Julia's face was a picture, but she wasn't the type to give up.

"Twenty," she said.

"Seventeen," said the man.

"We'll take it," said Tub.

Stick was counting on his fingers, trying to divide seventeen by five.

The shopkeeper reached into a drawer and counted out a bundle of notes.

"Anybody can make a mistake," he said, clearing the newspaper away. He lifted a crumpled sheet and leaned across to them again. "Now, something like this is really interesting," he said, waving the sheet at them.

George began to feel very uncomfortable. The headline stared at them. NEAR RIOT . . . but the man was pointing to the story above it.

"That's what you call really old," he was saying with his finger on a fuzzy picture.

They shifted to get a look at it, then George froze as he heard the unmistakable sound of something crunching. He hoped it was Tub's fizz bullets. He prayed it was Tub's fizz bullets, but he knew it wasn't. He forced himself to look.

It was impossible to tell what it had been. Now it was just a mass of broken glass under Kev's left foot. The shopkeeper kept calm. You could tell he was keeping calm by the way his knuckles had gone white from gripping the counter. The art history lesson was over.

"Just bring me the ticket," he said. Then he added, "Not you," as Kev made a move.

Julia picked up the little white ticket from among the fragments of glass and gave it to him.

"Twenty-five pounds," he said, and put the seventeen pounds back in the drawer. He pointed to the revolting notice. "You owe me eight pounds," he said.

They couldn't believe it. They had gone in there to make thousands and they ended up owing eight. It might as well have been thousands to them, for when they counted up, they had only one pound forty-three among them.

The man shook his head sadly. "It won't do," he said.

He shifted the vase onto a shelf behind him and George thought of making a quick burst for freedom. No use. They would probably end up breaking more things and not getting away. He laid the one pound forty-three on the counter.

"Look," he said, gathering up his Romeo costume, "you'll have to trust us to owe you it. We haven't got any more."

The man began to shake his head, then he put out a hand and extracted the frilly white blouse from George's bundle.

"Tell you what," he said, turning it over. "My wife sells antique clothes. This is a nice bit of lace. I'll take this and we'll call it quits."

George was about to say no way, or words to that effect, when he became aware of four pairs of eyes on him. He thought of what Sharon would say when he told her he'd lost half of his costume. He thought of explaining to the others that it was in fact his costume and not just rummage. The antiques dealer was speaking again.

"You can have your one pound forty-three back as well." That did it. If George refused, they would tear him limb from limb. There was a quick scramble as the money found its rightful owners. George picked up his share.

"It's a deal," he said.

There wasn't much to say on the way back to school, just the odd comment like, "It's a mug's game," from Tub, and "It nearly cost us money," from Stick.

George, Julia, and Kev didn't say anything in case Tub and Stick started blaming them.

They met Mr. Martin on their way into school and he gave them detention. They didn't even argue. George was so sunk in gloom that he nearly walked right past Sharon.

"Oh, George," she said brightly, "I meant to tell you last night to be very, very careful with the blouse I gave you. I really shouldn't have lent it because it belonged to my great-grandmother and is something of a family heirloom, but I did want you to look nice." George looked at her in horror.

"And, George, you will think again about the tights, won't you?"

She was gone before George could say anything, which was just as well, considering.

"Rummage," he muttered to himself. "I thought it was rummage. What's she going to say when she finds out I've sold her family heirloom?"

He thought of telling the others. No point in that—what could they do? He knew what Kev would say—what's an heirloom?

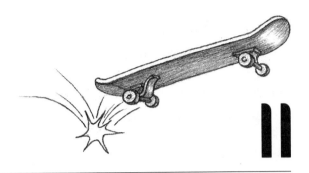

11

Geroge spent most of Friday avoiding Sharon and trying to figure out how to get the blouse back. Mr. Martin found him lurking behind a cabinet in his homeroom during afternoon break.

"You're not supposed to be in here, George," he said.

George tried to look ill, which wasn't all that hard.

"I'm not feeling too well," he said.

"Too many late nights?" said Mr. Martin. "You should be ashamed of yourself at your age. I hope you're better by tonight. I've arranged with the Sports Center to get the pool for an hour at seven o'clock. That should give you time to get back here and sort out the rummage for tomorrow."

George shuddered at the word "rummage" but Mr. Martin was collecting books and didn't notice.

"Oh, by the way," he said as he picked up the last of them, "Sharon was looking for you. Something about a dress rehearsal tomorrow night."

This time George didn't even have to try to look ill.

"Thanks," he said weakly, "I'll see her later."

"No, you won't," said Mr. Martin, "at least not until tonight. The headmaster has given her permission to go down to the local radio station this afternoon to give an interview about the fund-raising. We should get a good turnout tomorrow."

He cast a look in George's direction.

"You look fine," he said. "Go out and get some fresh air."

"I think I will," said George. "I'm feeling a lot better."

He had been let off the hook—he didn't have to face Sharon till seven.

The first person he met outside was Julia, looking like thunder.

"Have you heard?" she said.

"Oh, God, what now?" said George.

"Sharon and that interview," she went on. "Who arranged it? Who phoned the radio station? Me. And she goes to the head and gets him to send her.

What nerve."

"It doesn't matter who goes," said George. He really didn't mind Sharon's not being around at the moment.

Julia looked as if she were about to leap for his throat.

"It was a great idea though," he said quickly. "Terrific."

"You think so?" she said. "Well, I've got an even better one."

"What's that?" said George.

Julia smiled.

"Think I'm going to tell you? You'd just go blabbing to Sharon. Just wait and see." And with that she was gone.

Maybe he should have forced her to tell him what she was up to, but he couldn't be bothered. He didn't have long to enjoy himself. Just until seven o'clock. Oddly enough, when seven o'clock came, he had other things on his mind. Stick, Tub, and Julia were waiting outside the Sports Center when he got there. Kev was the last to arrive. It was the sight of him pushing a baby carriage around the corner that drove everything else from George's mind. Kev's left arm seemed to be in a cast. What now, thought George, looking at the carriage. There wasn't a baby in Kev's family.

"It's the gnome," said Kev before they could ask.

"I thought you hated that gnome," said Tub. "Why are you taking it for a walk?"

"Dad says I've got to get rid of it," said Kev.

"At the Sports Center?" said Stick. "What are you going to do with it? Enroll it in a karate class?"

A voice spoke from his left elbow.

"It's never too early to start, or too late," said a little old lady. "That's where I'm going. Karate. You're not safe on the streets these days."

She peered nearsightedly into the carriage.

"That baby is rigid with cold," she said, patting the blanket that covered the gnome. "You'd better get it inside." Then she tottered up the steps to the center.

Julia looked after her. "Karate? She can barely walk."

George stuck to the point. "Why does he want you to get rid of it?"

Kev scratched his head with his good arm.

"It was after we came back from the hospital," he said. "He put the gnome in this old carriage and said he never wanted to see it again, so I brought it along. I'll take it to school later. It can go in the rummage sale." The others looked at each other. Nobody wanted to ask.

"What were you doing at the hospital?" said George.

"Getting this cast put on," said Kev.

They waited. Kev didn't seem to be going to say any more.

The Sports Center door opened and Sharon appeared.

"Oh, George . . ." she began. George trembled. Now he was in for it. But she caught sight of Kev.

"What happened to your arm, Kevin?"

"Accident," said Kev. "At least it wasn't my fault. If that old guy hadn't yelled at me, I wouldn't have missed the gnome and hit that water pipe. It's only a hairline fracture."

"The arm or the water pipe?" said George.

"Missed the gnome?" said Sharon.

"With the pickax," said Kev.

Sharon looked as if she wanted to ask something else but didn't know what. At least it had put George and the dress rehearsal out of her mind for the moment.

Mr. Martin appeared around the corner.

"All right, let's go, then," he said. "Oh, by the way, Kev, I hope nothing's wrong at your house. The garden seems to be under a lot of water, but I see the fire engines are there. Glad to see you're looking after the baby. I didn't know you had a new addition to the family." He sprinted up the steps. "Come on, Sharon, we've got to get the timekeepers organized."

They helped Kev up the steps with the carriage while he told them about the man who had chased him from the old house when he went to get the pickax.

"It was only a rusty old pickax," he said. "I thought

I had gotten away, then he turns up in the backyard. 'Mindless vandalism,' he yells. No wonder I missed the gnome. He gave me the fright of my life."

The next problem was where to put the gnome. They got past the reception desk. The old woman was arguing with the man at the desk about the discount for senior citizens. He just waved them on and got back to the old lady. George guessed she didn't need karate. She could talk anybody to death.

The dressing rooms were empty by the time they got down.

"That's okay, then," said George. "We can leave it here. So long as we're finished first, we can get back down and get it out before anybody sees it."

"Why bother?" said Tub. "The man at the desk's not bothered."

"The man at the desk's not the problem," said George. "The headmaster's the problem. Do you want to try explaining to him why we've brought a concrete gnome in a baby carriage into the Sports Center?"

Tub tried to think what he would say to the headmaster.

"I'm hurrying," he said after a moment, and started throwing clothes in all directions.

"They'll be started already," said Stick, doing the same.

"Not a chance," said George through a mouthful of sweater. "They'll have a speech from the head about water safety and doing it for the school and all that stuff first."

"Can somebody tie my plastic bag on?" said Kev.

Stick was hopping on one foot, getting into his swimming trunks. "You can't go in the water with your arm in a cast."

"I can if I tie a plastic bag around it," said Kev.

"You're mad," said Tub. "It'll dissolve."

"Look, we haven't time to argue," said George. "Let's have the bag, Kev."

Julia was waiting for them when they got out of their dressing room, and they pelted down the corridor to the pool.

"No running," yelled an attendant as they rounded a corner and cannoned into two men coming the other way. They walked on, leaving the attendant explaining to the men that only students were allowed in the dressing room area during the sponsored snorkel and heading them off toward the seats.

The head was just finishing his pep talk when they arrived. Surprisingly, the sponsored snorkel had been really popular and the sides of the pool were crammed with kids.

"Four lengths each at most," Mr. Martin was saying. "Or else we won't have time to let everybody have a turn. Now, who are the first five?"

"Us," said George before anyone else could get in a word. Mr. Martin looked at Kev.

"Why have you got a plastic bag on your arm, Kev?"

"Protection," said Kev. "In case the cast gets wet."

"You can't swim with your arm in a cast," said Sharon. "I'll take his place, George."

George looked at her. She had just finished fixing the dividing ropes for the lanes and was still in the water. It was difficult, maybe the hardest thing he had ever done in his life. She was wearing a blue bathing suit that exactly matched her eyes, and her hair was kind of floating. She looked like a mermaid.

"No thanks," said George. "Kev'll be okay."

There was no way they could have Sharon free to go down to the dressing room with them—too risky.

"You go with the second group," he finished.

He couldn't believe it. He had actually turned Sharon down. Her head went up and she looked at him as if he'd just turned into a toad again.

"All right, but I must see you later about the dress rehearsal. For the sake of the concert, you understand."

George understood only too well.

"Come on, wimp," said Julia in his ear.

They did their lengths in record time and Kev got a special cheer when he came out. He'd done the whole thing with the plastic bag sticking up in the air. It was amazing. He took the bag off as he came out of the pool and waved the cast at the spectators. They went wild. Then he looked at his fingers.

"What does it mean when your fingers turn blue, I mean really blue?" he said.

Mr. Martin looked at them. "It means somebody tied that plastic bag too tight and cut off the blood to your hand."

"Is that bad?" said Kev.

"Depends if you ever want to use it again," said Mr. Martin.

"Come on, Kev," said Julia. "We've got to go."

"What about my hand?" said Kev.

"Your hand will be all right," said Stick. "Will you come on."

They got dressed as quickly as they could and wheeled the baby carriage out into the corridor.

"You go and see if there's anybody around," said George to Stick.

He was back a moment later.

"No go," he said. "The head's in the front hall talking to some people. We can't wheel it past him. He's sure to stop us and ask questions."

"Who's he talking to?" said Julia.

"I don't know. Just people."

"What kind of people?" She seemed really interested.

"Why do you want to know?" asked George, suspicious.

"Because I do," said Julia. "I'll be back in a minute." She disappeared around the corner.

"What's she up to?" said George. He had remembered what she had said that morning about having another idea. She was back in a moment, beaming.

"They came," she said.

"Who came?" said George.

"The TV people. I got in touch with them. Said it was great local news and it just so happens they're doing a program about education cuts. They said they would send somebody tonight."

"How do you know it's them?" said Tub.

Julia looked at him scornfully. "They're wearing leather jackets and jeans and the head's being nice to them. They must be TV people."

This seemed to settle it as far as the rest were concerned, so George left it at that.

"Look," he said, "we're going to have to find another way out with this gnome."

Suddenly a voice said behind them, "If you're looking for an easier way out with the carriage, I've just passed an emergency exit."

He was a tall man, wearing a suit, so according to Julia's theory he couldn't be a TV person. Maybe he was the director or somebody important. There was another, smaller man behind him. They were smiling. Maybe if they were TV people after all, they would understand about concrete gnomes.

"Thanks very much," said George.

The two men led them back down the corridor and around a couple of corners.

"In there," said the taller one. "There's an exit just

behind that control panel. Maybe you'd better see if there's room enough to get the carriage around."

"Oh, right," said George, and they crowded in.

The room was very small.

"I don't see any exit," Tub was saying when they heard the door click shut. Darkness descended. It was pitch black.

"Who shut the door?" said Stick.

"I can't see a thing," said Julia.

"Where's the light switch?" said George.

They found it at last and switched on the light. Tub was right. There was no exit. Nobody would admit to shutting the door, and when they tried it, it wouldn't open. They shook it and rattled it and kicked it in exasperation. Finally Kev hit it with his cast and winced.

"A lot of good that'll do," said Julia.

George looked at Kev's reddening fingers.

"At least it's brought the blood back to his hand," he said.

"I think it's broken," said Kev.

"Lucky it's in a cast, then, isn't it," said Julia. "Look, what I can't understand is why those men haven't opened the door from the outside."

"Maybe they didn't wait around after we came in here," said Stick.

"We were yelling and banging on the door," said George. "They'd have heard that even if they had gone down the corridor."

"Maybe they locked us in," said Tub.

George gave him a look.

"Too many comics—like I said before."

"What are we going to do?" said Julia.

"Shout till somebody hears us," said Stick. "Somebody's bound to hear us. Right, Tub?"

Tub clamped his lips together, then said, "You don't want my opinion. I get them all out of comics. Ask brainbox George."

George didn't seem to be listening.

"George?" said Stick.

"What?"

"We yell, okay?"

"Wait a minute," he said. "I've been trying to picture where we are."

"Locked in a storeroom," said Tub. "Any idiot can tell you that—even idiots that read comics."

Tub was a bit upset.

"No, I mean, if you think of the way we came in," said George, "we must be at the other end of the building from the dressing rooms. There didn't seem to be much at this end but storage closets. I wouldn't bet on anybody's being down this way tonight."

"I'm not staying here all night," said Julia. "Think of something."

"I'm trying," said George. "If you'd all shut up and give me a chance, I might be able to."

Silence. Four pairs of eyes fastened on him expectantly. It was worse than the shouting. George couldn't bear to look at them. His eyes scoured the room, no more than just a big closet. They came to rest on the control panel. He moved toward it. Anything was better than staring at the others. It looked like a fairly complicated setup with switches and levers and things. One was for the lighting, another seemed to have something to do with draining the pool, and another one was for the wave machine. A plan began to form in George's mind.

"What's the time?" he said.

"Five to eight," said Stick.

"They'll just be finishing in the pool," said George. "We had it only till eight, right?"

"Right," said Stick. "What's the idea?"

"This," said George, pointing to a label above one of the levers. "It's worth a try."

They crowded around and he watched their faces as they saw what he meant to do.

"What do you say?" he said.

They looked at each other, then Julia said, "Go ahead. Pull it."

George pulled the lever under the label that said WAVE MACHINE/MASTER SWITCH OVERRIDE.

They didn't have long to wait after that. The first face they saw when the door opened was Mr. Martin's. It was closely followed by an irate attendant.

"I might have known," said Mr. Martin.

"Kids," said the attendant, pushing the lever back up. "Horsing around. It's a disgrace. You ought to be banned from the center. I'll complain to the school, you see if I don't. Kids. Just wait till I find your headmaster." He waddled off down the corridor.

"He ought to be a school janitor," said George.

Mr. Martin was just standing there looking at him, which was odd, because by rights he should have been shouting at them.

"What I can't understand is how you could padlock yourselves in," he said.

George looked at the padlock in Mr. Martin's hand.

"No wonder we couldn't get out," he said.

"Who did it?" said Mr. Martin.

"I bet it was those two men," said Tub.

George kicked him. He didn't want Mr. Martin asking awkward questions about why they had been looking for another way out.

"What men?" said Mr. Martin.

"Don't pay any attention to him. He reads too many comics," said George. Tub looked as if he were going to blow a fuse, but George continued. "The padlock must have clicked shut when the door closed."

"What were you doing in there anyway?" said Mr. Martin. "Have you any idea of the chaos you caused? One minute the last group is finishing off, the next they're swamped with waves and all the other kids jump in, thinking it's a party."

"It was the only way to attract attention," said George. "I thought if this was the master switch, somebody would have to come down to turn it off. It wasn't our fault we were locked in."

"I'm not so sure of that, George," said Mr. Martin, "but I haven't got time to argue with you. I'll have to go and find the headmaster before that attendant does. Maybe I can smooth things over, maybe not, but in either case I advise you to keep out of his way tonight."

He snapped the padlock back on the door.

"Activating the wave machine. Why couldn't you just shout like normal people?"

"We tried that," said Stick, "and it didn't work. We just used our initiative."

Mr. Martin said something unrepeatable about initiative and George wondered whether getting out of taking the school trip was worth all this trouble to him.

"Sorry, sir," he said.

"So am I, George, so am I," he replied, and ran off to deal with the headmaster.

"Thank goodness that's over," said Stick. "Let's get out of here."

"Wait a minute," said George.

"What?" said Tub. "And if you start talking about me and comics, I'll brain you."

"We've lost the gnome," said George.

They all looked around as if they expected the baby carriage to materialize suddenly in front of them.

"What do we do?" said Stick. "We can't go around asking people if they've seen a concrete gnome in a baby carriage."

They had begun to trudge toward the main hall when around the corner came a strange apparition. It was gray-haired and elderly and dressed in a karate outfit several times too big for it but, more important, it was wheeling a baby carriage.

"There you are," said the old lady. "I've been looking for you everywhere. When I saw those men going off with your baby, I knew they were up to no good." She seemed out of breath, but she chuckled just the same. "Wait till I tell my niece. She says I'm too old for karate. Too old. Why, I hardly got started on them before they ran away. I haven't looked at the baby yet. I hope it's all right. The blanket seems to have slipped over its little face."

She reached over to pull back the blanket and they moved as one. It couldn't have been better if they had rehearsed it. George got between her and the carriage. Kev yanked the carriage toward him and turned it around. Stick and Tub moved to either side of it, and Julia took the old lady's arm and began to ask her about karate chops.

George was proud of them. What a team!

She was still saying what a good baby it must be and how it hadn't cried at all, when they deposited her at the karate class again.

"I just slipped out to go to the ladies' room," she said as they left her. "Who would have thought a thing like that would happen? Just wait till I tell my niece."

The headmaster was in the front hall with Mr. Martin, so the group had to wait till they had gone. They stationed themselves and the carriage behind some dismantled trampolines.

"We'll have to get back to the school and sort out the rummage," said Tub.

George was more concerned about getting out of the Sports Center alive. It was unlucky for him that he peered around the corner just as Sharon crossed the front hall. The headmaster had gone.

"Oh, George, I'll walk back to school with you and we can discuss the rehearsal," she said.

He heard the sniggering behind him and kicked the nearest leg. Tub yelped.

"The head's still there," he lied. "Give it another five minutes and I'll see you back at school. My cover's blown anyway."

If there was one thing he would not put up with, it was walking back to school with Sharon *and* the rest.

"Hi, Sharon," he said breezily, "I was just looking for you."

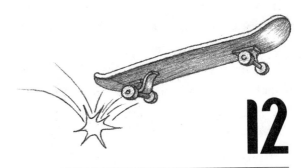

12

By the time the others arrived at the school, the sorting of the rummage was well in hand. George wasn't feeling too bad either. Sharon hadn't mentioned the blouse, and he had arranged to have a dress rehearsal after the rummage sale. They would surely take in quite a bit of money at the rummage sale, and if anybody deserved a percentage of the profits, he was the one. A quick trip to the antiques shop to buy back the blouse and then to Sharon's for the rehearsal.

And he had handled the question of the tights not too badly either. He hadn't actually said he would wear them, but then again, he hadn't said he wouldn't. She had smiled at him when she gave him the tights. The Sharon situation could have been worse. The skateboard situation wasn't so good, but there was the concert still to come.

He was standing there, looking at a pair of long black tights, when the others arrived. He rolled them up quickly and stuffed them in his pocket. No need to give the rest a reason for mocking him.

Sharon was in an efficient mood, and by the time Mr. Martin got there, they had nearly finished. He drew George aside.

"Talk about luck," he said. "The headmaster didn't even hear about your incident with the wave machine."

"But that attendant went off to find him," said George. Mr. Martin nodded.

"He didn't stand a chance. You know there were TV people there?"

"Julia fixed it up," said George.

"Good for Julia, then. They saved your skin."

"How?"

"Look, George," said Mr. Martin, "wherever TV people go, idiots leap out of the woodwork wanting to be on the box. Well, the word seems to have gotten around pretty quickly that they were there, and this old woman in a karate outfit arrives talking about having rescued a baby from kidnapers. Kidnapers, I ask you. Have you ever heard anything more ridiculous?"

George swallowed.

"What happened?"

"They phoned her niece, that's what happened. She came and took her aunt away. Honestly, it's just so irresponsible, letting elderly people do things like karate. She must have gotten a bump on the head. Jenny says that's the last time she's going. She was against it from the start.

"Jenny?" said George.

Mr. Martin coughed. "The niece," he said. "Nice girl. She's a social worker."

George decided not to ask any more. Better to quit while he was ahead, and thanks to the old woman, he was definitely ahead. If Mr. Martin wanted to get mixed up with somebody who had a karate-crazed senior citizen for an aunt, that was his business.

"What did the TV people say?" he asked.

"They've talked to the head," said Mr. Martin, "and they're going to do some interviews at the concert tomorrow night. They seem quite pleased actually. They were looking for what they called a human interest angle for their program on education cuts."

George could feel the sweat standing out on his forehead.

"They're not going to film the concert, are they?"

He could just imagine it. Bad enough to have to do this Shakespeare thing, but putting it on television. It was too much.

The rest had heard him. They were around like flies.

"Who's filming?"

"Are we going to be on TV?"

"You'll have to wear the tights, George. Make it look really professional."

"You were on the radio. It's my turn to be on TV."

"Quiet, quiet," said Mr. Martin. "It'll probably be only a couple of minutes at the end of the program. Nothing to get excited about."

"We'll put it on the posters," said Sharon. "It'll be a sellout."

"Like church services on TV," said Tub. "My mom says it's a disgrace. People go only because they'll be on television."

"Think of the ticket money," said Stick in George's ear.

But George could think only of the tights and the frilly blouse.

It wasn't until they were about to leave that George realized that something was missing—again.

"Where's the gnome?" he said to Kev.

"At the Sports Center," said Kev. "We forgot it."

"Forgot it?" said George. "How could you forget it? You were standing there with it when I left."

"It was after that old woman arrived and everybody started shouting," said Julia. "We thought we'd better slip out quietly."

"Without the gnome?" said George.

"I thought Tub had it," said Stick.

"I thought you had it," said Kev to Stick.

George stopped them before the argument degenerated into a brawl.

"Somebody will have to go back for it."

"Not tonight," said Julia. "I'm sick of that gnome. No wonder you hate it, Kev."

It was agreed that Kev and Stick would go back for it in the morning, and George left it at that. It had been a busy day.

When he got home, George found the old vacuum cleaner tied up, waiting in the hall for him to take to the rummage sale. Bits of grass and weed still showed poking out of various tubes. His mother had bought a carpet sweeper. That didn't make him feel any better either. If they had been able to afford a new vacuum cleaner, she would have bought one, wouldn't she?

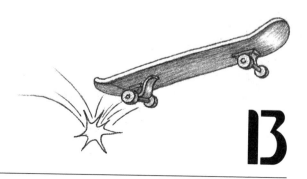

When George and his friends arrived at the auditorium the next day, it looked like a war zone. The way things had been going, they shouldn't have been all that surprised. Mr. Hughes, the janitor, was having every kind of fit.

"Window smashed as well," he was saying. "I tell you—kids today, they ought to be locked up, the lot of them. And who knows what else they've done. I'll need to go and check the rest of the school now and me with the bowling club finals in half an hour. It's a disgrace, that's what it is, a disgrace I want this place cleaned up by the time I get back."

He went off, still muttering, and left them in peace to look at the devastation. Tables were overturned. Clothes, books, toys, furniture—everything lay jumbled on the floor.

George stood there with his mother's vacuum cleaner in his hands.

"It was all in nice neat piles when we left last night," wailed Julia.

"Who would want to break into a rummage sale?" said Tub.

"I suppose we're going to have to clean it up," said George. It looked worse than his bedroom on a bad day.

"I don't suppose that vacuum cleaner's working," Julia said.

George shook his head. "It's all jammed up with weeds. I don't think it'll ever work again."

"We've got only half an hour before the doors open," said Sharon.

"It's not fair," said Tub. "We didn't do it."

"No," said Sharon, "but we're responsible for the rummage sale, so there's no use moaning. Come on." She started to heave the nearest table upright. George looked at her in admiration and went to help. The others followed. Sharon smiled at George.

"I'll leave this to you, George," she said. "You're much stronger than I am. I'll just go and set up the table at the front door."

"Me Tarzan, you Jane," said Julia sourly as she disappeared.

It was nearly done by the time Kev and Stick arrived with the baby carriage.

"Trust you to miss the work," said Julia.

"Any trouble getting the gnome out?" said George. Kev grunted. He was heaving the gnome into an upright position in the carriage. It looked kind of weird.

"That doesn't look much like a gnome," said Tub.

"Horrible, isn't it?" Kev said with satisfaction.

Julia was looking puzzled.

"I've seen that before," she said.

"You saw it last night," said Stick.

"I didn't," said Julia. "It was all bundled up. I mean, I've seen it somewhere else."

"Yuk," George said. "In a horror film maybe."

They all looked at the gnome. It had a sneering kind of wizened face and horns and, instead of feet, it had hooves. It was horrible.

"Nobody is going to buy that, Kev," said Tub. "You're wasting your time. You'll have to take it home again."

"I can't take it home," said Kev. "My dad says he never wants to see it again, and besides, somebody might buy it. There were two men at the house last night when I was out, asking if we had any garden statues for sale. Mom told them they had just missed this, so maybe they'll come to the sale and buy it."

Something flitted across the back of George's mind, but Sharon came in to announce she was going to open the doors, and he let it go.

He pushed the carriage behind a wardrobe. It was upsetting looking at that thing. Sharon took up her place at the door, collecting the five-pence entrance charge and they got started. It was quite a success. For one thing, everybody's mother came and bought something. George watched the growing pile of money with satisfaction. At least they would get the percentage this time. He had not forgotten the blouse.

Mr. Martin looked in to see if everything was all right. The headmaster turned up briefly and Sharon dealt with him. George sold a pair of roller skates to Amanda for seventy-five pence. They were old ones of his. Every so often the wheels locked and pitched you forward. He had stopped wearing them even before they got too small for him. He enjoyed selling them to Amanda. The only black spot was Stick's mother turning up with the dog and leaving it.

"Maybe we could sell it," said Tub.

Stick groaned and tied its leash to the baby carriage. It jumped up and put its paws on the side of the carriage and saw the gnome. Immediately it began to howl. Tub threw it a fizz bullet and it calmed down.

"Amazing how it likes those things," said Stick. "I wonder what's in them."

Tub looked at the one he was just going to eat, then put it back in the paper bag.

They had been going for about an hour and a half and the money was mounting up nicely when it happened. Julia was wrapping up a stack of saucers for a customer when she gave a squeal.

"I knew I had seen it somewhere before," she said. "Look, look, you guys."

She tore off a corner of the newspaper and thrust the half-wrapped saucers at the customer. The others looked at her in amazement. Her eyes were shining and she was almost dancing.

"Look," she said again, shoving the paper under their noses. "It's valuable. It says so here. There's even a reward. And you said this couldn't happen."

The rush had died down. The woman with the saucers left, giving Julia a funny look. They were the only ones in the auditorium.

"What are you talking about?" said George, eyeing the money box. Now was the moment. No customers. Sharon outside at the front door.

"Only that Kev's gnome isn't a gnome. It's the statue that's been missing from the museum for the last three months, and it's valuable."

"You're crazy."

"You're kidding."

"Not again, Julia."

"Kev, have you been stealing from the museum?"

Tub started to say something about *Antiques Road-show* and what his mother said—again.

They all looked at the paper. It was a bit crumpled and the photograph was smudgy, but it was the gnome all right. There couldn't be two of them.

"I knew I'd seen it before. Remember the antiques dealer pointed it out to us," Julia was saying when two men walked in.

Tub had started to say hello when the taller one reached across and snatched the paper out of Julia's hand.

"So the penny finally dropped, did it?" he said.

The thought that had flitted through George's mind came back and hit him like a hammer. Break-in at the school last night, two men at Kev's house asking about statues, two men at the Sports Center locking them in the control room. It was the same two men.

"Okay, where is it?" said the tall one.

Nobody even tried saying "where's what?" Not even Kev.

George leapt for the carriage. Luckily there was a trestle table between him and the two men. He grabbed the handle of the carriage and pushed.

"Catch," he yelled to Stick as the carriage went hurtling across the floor. The dog, still tied to the handle, yelped as it tried to keep up. The gnome lurched and slid down among the blankets. Stick

119

caught the carriage. He also caught on to the idea.

"Catch," he yelled in turn to Tub as the men made for him, and the carriage went hurtling once more across the room. It was unlucky that in the game of catch-the-carriage Kev was passing to Julia. Being small, she nearly got run over, but the dog saved the day. As the smaller man leapt for the carriage, he tripped over the leash, which was stretched out tight with the dog panting on the end. By this time those not involved in the catching of the carriage had come up with the idea of getting up on the tables and throwing anything they could find at the enemy.

It was this scene that met the janitor's eye when he walked in. George thought he would burst. His face went purple and he could hardly speak. When he did, his language was terrible. George thought of trying to explain to him, but that wasn't a very good idea. The janitor wasn't the listening type at the best of times. Right now he was concentrating on being heard. The two men just happened to be on top of a table, and the janitor advanced on them, waving a broom and shouting about setting an example. They wouldn't get a better chance to make a break for it.

"Out," yelled George, and they made a dive for the door.

The dog was a nuisance, tied to the carriage. George scooped it up and threw it in beside the gnome. It howled and tried to get out, but by this

time they were building up a good speed and it shrank back and cowered in terror under the blanket. Sharon rose as they passed, her mouth open.

"Hi, Sharon," said George. "Just taking the dog for a walk." They hurtled past.

There was a crash behind them as the janitor and the two men burst into the corridor and bumped slap-bang into Sharon. Her table fell over and George heard the sound of money scattering in all directions. He had a sudden, intensely painful vision of all that rummage-sale money lying in the box in the hall—intact, untouched. Missed it again, he thought. The skateboard began to look doubtful.

They were halfway down the street before the two men broke free of the janitor and Sharon. George glanced quickly behind him. It wouldn't take them long to catch up, not out in the open. What they needed was cover.

"Into the park," he roared, and steered the carriage drunkenly through the gates. Delaying tactics—that's what they needed. Time to plan. Where in the park? The fountain, where they always went. No good, too open. Then again, maybe . . . A plan began to form in George's mind.

"Fountain," he gasped. He was almost out of breath.

Nobody argued. They wove their way in and out of pathways till they got there. They wouldn't be that easy to follow.

"Get the cherub, Kev," said George.

"What for?" said Kev.

"I've got this plan. Go on, Kev, you're the only one that's fit."

It was true. He wasn't even breathing hard. Kev went to get the cherub while the others stood around trying to get their breath. Julia was the first to recover.

"What's the plan, then?"

"We swap the cherub for the gnome," said George, "then we let them see us, lead them away from the scene, dump the cherub, and then come back for the gnome."

"Sounds crazy," said Stick.

"Well, it isn't," said George. "You put something in a really obvious place right out in the open and nobody looks twice at it. We let them see us trying to hide the cherub, they think it's the gnome, right size, right kind of shape. We run away. They won't be interested in us. By the time they discover it's the cherub and not the gnome, we'll be long gone. It's logical."

"And you've got the nerve to say I read too many comics?" said Tub.

"Will somebody give Kev a hand?" said Julia. "He's in a cast, remember?"

They were a bit wet by the time they got the cherub and the gnome switched.

"It looks quite good up there," said Stick. "Lucky that cherub was loose."

"That wasn't luck. I've been throwing stones at it for years," said George.

"What about the dog?" Tub said.

It didn't look any happier sharing the carriage with the cherub.

"Leave it where it is," said George. "It'll just get in the way otherwise."

The trick now was to get some distance from the fountain, then let themselves be seen. They were creeping around the back of the tennis courts when there was a yell from the other side.

"We've been found out," said Stick.

"Let's go, then," said George.

"Where?"

"Out of the park for a start," said Julia.

They took the lower road out over the common. As they passed the remains of the cub hut, Tub suggested leaving the cherub there. George looked back. The enemy was in sight. He hesitated.

"No. Too open," he said. "They'd discover the switch too soon and be after us again."

He looked around for a hiding place. The common was depressingly open. Then down at the far end he caught sight of the old house.

"How about there, in the house?" he said. "We'll stash it in that closet where you found the vase, then let them see us running away without it. It'll take them a while to find it, and that'll give us time to go back for the gnome."

They pounded off across the common toward the house. The carriage rocked and bounced. The dog kept its head down. Only the odd yelp told them it was still there.

It was the dog that was their undoing. Or, to be more exact, the undoing of the dog. With all the running and bouncing, the knot on its leash had worked itself tight.

"Cut it," said Tub, hopping from foot to foot.

"What with?" said Stick.

"Unclip the leash," said George.

"I need the leash or the dog will run away," said Stick, concentrating on the knot. "Wait a minute. I think I've got it."

"Wrong," said a voice from the door. "You've had it."

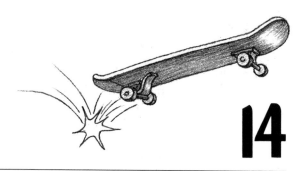

14

They stood in the doorway looking like the Incredible Hulk and a Munchkin.

"Okay," said the big one, "let's have no more nonsense and you won't get hurt."

Nonsense was the last thing on George's mind. He got the feeling the big guy meant what he said.

Tub tried to get into the closet and out of the way as the two men bore down on them. The taller one wrenched the blanket off the carriage and the dog yelped and bared its teeth. It was a puny effort, but the man drew his hand back quickly. George made a mental note that he did not like dogs, even insignificant ones tied up to baby carriages.

"That's not it, Joe," said the smaller one, looking at the cherub.

"Shut up, Fred," said Joe. "I told you, no names."

No names, thought George. They weren't exactly the brains of Britain.

"Where's the statue, then?" said Joe.

Nobody answered.

"Want me to persuade them?" said Fred.

Joe shook his head. "No rough stuff," he said.

George's spirits lifted.

"Not yet," Joe continued.

George's spirits fell.

"We're not telling you," said George. "You can do what you like to us, but we won't tell."

It sounded good, and he didn't think his voice had been shaking.

"What?" Tub squeaked.

"Oh, come on, George," said Stick. "I'm no hero even if you fancy yourself as one."

"He's right," said Julia, coming unexpectedly to George's rescue. She turned to the men. "You're thieves," she said, "and thugs, threatening to beat up children."

George looked at her in amazement. It wasn't so much her standing up to them—just that nobody had called Julia a child for years and got away with it.

"And if anybody else talks," she went on, "they'll have me to deal with."

Even the dog cringed. With Julia in this mood, nobody was going to argue.

"Who me?" said Stick.

"Never crossed my mind," said Tub sadly.

"How did you know we had it anyway?" said Kev to the men.

"You were seen," said Joe, "attacking it with a pickax. Do you realize how much it's worth?" He seemed quite upset.

"No," said Kev. "How much?"

"Look," said Fred, "we haven't got all day to stand here jawing. Let me rough them up."

Joe seemed to consider it this time.

"It wouldn't look good," said George, "beating up kids."

He could see Joe thinking about it, Fred too.

"Into the closet," said Fred.

They got into the closet. Fred pushed the carriage in after them.

"We'll leave you to think it over," he said. "See how you feel in a few hours' time."

They heard the sound of a key turning in the lock.

"That guy's sick," said Tub. "He's got a mania for locking people in closets."

"Maybe it's just us," said George. "Maybe we bring it out in him."

There was silence for a moment, then George spoke again.

"How come he had a key for this closet? I didn't see one in the lock before."

"This must be where they stash their stuff," said Kev.

"How d'you mean?" said George.

"Stands to reason," said Kev. "I mean, this is where my dad found the gnome in the first place, only the closet wasn't locked. He thought it was just junk. Brought it home for Mom."

"They must have left it here till the heat died down," said Tub.

"Comics again?" said George.

"You should talk," said Tub. "Look where your idea got us."

"There was nothing wrong with my idea," said George. "I mean, if Kev had said this was where the gnome came from, I wouldn't have suggested bringing it back here, would I? No wonder they got here so fast."

Tub had been lost in thought. "The guy who chased you with the pickax must have told them where you lived," he said now.

"He didn't have the pickax," said Kev. "I had the pickax."

"It doesn't matter who had the pickax," said Tub. "The point is, who was that guy that chased you?"

"I don't know," said Kev. "Just a guy with a hard hat and a clipboard."

"Must be from the council," said George. "They all go around with hard hats and clipboards. They must be going to demolish this place soon."

"And that's why those two came back for the gnome," said Stick. "When they heard it was going to be knocked down at last."

All this time Julia hadn't said a word. It must have been a strain on her, for now she exploded.

"We should be trying to get out of here instead of standing around talking."

"How?" said Stick.

"George?" said Julia.

George shook his head. "Don't ask me."

"What's wrong with you?" Tub said to him. "Where are all the bright ideas?"

But George had no bright ideas—for once.

"Look around," he said. "The door's solid, the walls are thick, even the floor's in good condition. It must be the only part of the house that isn't falling down, and we have to be stuck in it. Why don't we just save our strength, wait till they come back, and make a break for it."

"*If* they come back," said Stick.

"They'll come back," said George.

Two hours later he wasn't so sure. It was all very well saying they would leave them to think it over, but this was ridiculous. He had visions of Fred and Joe being in an accident, lying in a hospital somewhere, unconscious. Nobody would know they were here. They would never get out. In years to come there would just be a pile of bones and dust. Unless the house got knocked down around them. Then the bones would be dust too.

Tub was moaning again about being hungry. They had eaten all the fizz bullets but five. They were saving those for an emergency. Funny how your idea of what was an emergency changed when you were locked in a closet, George thought. He leaned back against the wall and closed his eyes. Everything went black. It was several moments before he realized this was important. He opened his eyes again. Yes, he could see dimly, but it still wasn't completely dark. He closed his eyes again, just to be sure. Blackness.

"It's not completely dark in here," he said.

"If you're trying to cheer us up, don't bother," said Stick, "not if that's the best you can do."

"It should be completely dark," said George.

"Well, it isn't. Don't knock it," said Stick.

"There are no windows," said George.

"Look, George," said Tub, "we know you mean well, but will you just shut up. It's bad enough being locked in here with the dog without you going raving mad as well."

"The dog's got claustrophobia," said Stick.

"I thought it was agoraphobia," said Tub.

"That was last week," said Stick.

George's eyes were turned up, looking at the ceiling.

"The one place we didn't think of," he said.

Julia followed his eyes.

"Light," she yelled, grabbing Kev. "Light."

"Light what?" said Kev. "I haven't got any matches."

"Light nothing, dope," she said. "Look, there's light coming through that hole in the ceiling."

"Not much," said Tub. His voice was casual, but you could tell he was interested by the way he was trying to climb on Stick's shoulders.

"Get off," said Stick.

"You're the tallest," said Tub.

"Kev's the strongest," Stick said.

Everybody dived for Kev. He had never been so popular.

George got them sorted out. "Julia on Kev's shoulders. She's the lightest and smallest."

The ceiling was quite high, but Julia could reach the hole. Her head disappeared.

"What's up there, Julia?"

"Another closet," said Julia. "The floor's rotten, just a few beams above this ceiling."

Stick groaned. "Just our luck, another closet."

"Not a locked one, idiot," said Julia. "The door's open. That's where the light is coming from."

"What are you waiting for, then?" yelled Tub.

"The hole isn't big enough for me to get through," she said.

"You're the smallest. It'll have to be you," George said. "Try knocking away part of the ceiling. Even a little would be enough. You're so skinny."

"I'll get you for that, George Aitken," came Julia's voice.

Perhaps anger lent strength to her elbow, or maybe she meant what she said. In any event, they heard her fist connect with the plaster and then the ceiling fell in. There was a yell from Julia and they looked up, eyes smarting, choking. As the dust began to settle, they could see her legs dangling in the air.

"Kev," she yelled. "Where are you? This beam's going." True enough, the beam she was holding on to with what looked like her fingernails was beginning to sag and creak. Kev lumbered to his feet just in time. At the same time it seemed his shoulders were under her feet, the beam snapped and she was gone, scrambling up through the hole.

They all held their breath, waiting for the impact as she fell down again. Nothing happened.

"Julia?" said George.

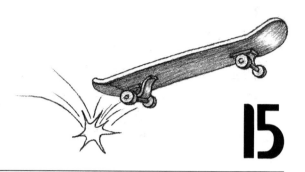

"I'm okay." Julia's voice drifted down to them, slightly muffled. "I think I've swallowed some plaster."

"You shouldn't have had your mouth open," said Tub, picking bits of ceiling out of his hair.

"I was screaming at the time," said Julia. "It comes from being scared."

Her voice was stronger now.

"Hurry up and let us out," yelled George. "They could be back anytime."

George's imagination had transferred Fred and Joe from their hospital beds to the front doorstep.

"I'm going," she yelled back, her voice receding. The rest looked at each other. They were covered in plaster dust. The dog shook itself and a fine film of dust rose in the air and started them coughing again. There was a rattling at the door and somebody kicked it.

"The key's not here," said Julia.

"They must have taken it with them," said Tub. "Isn't that typical?"

"How rotten can you get?" said Stick.

"Break it down," said Tub.

"Look, bonehead, if you can't break it down from your side, I can't break it down from mine. George?"

"What?"

"What are we going to do?"

"I hate that question," said George.

He pondered.

"George?" yelled Julia.

"Shut up. He's thinking," Stick yelled back.

They stood there in respectful silence while George thought. He looked at the hole in the ceiling. There were still some beams that seemed to be intact up there. If only they had a rope of some kind. He dug his hands deep in his pockets. It was funny. In all the time he had spent in the closet, it hadn't once occurred to him that he had missed the dress rehearsal with Sharon. It was the tights that reminded him. His eyes lit up.

"He's thought of something," Tub roared through the door to Julia.

"What?"

"Julia," said George. "Go up and see if you can find something, anything in that closet that will take Kev's weight."

"Why me?" said Kev suspiciously as they listened to Julia clattering back up the stairs.

"Because you're the heaviest," said George. Kev still looked suspicious.

Julia's head appeared above them. She started hammering on the beams. The beams began to crumble.

"Watch it," said Tub as a piece came crashing down on them.

"The beams are no good," said Julia.

"You don't say?" said Stick.

"Try to find something strong that you can tie a rope to," said George.

"I haven't got a rope," said Julia.

"No, but I have," said George. "Go on, Julia, get a move on."

"Where did you get a rope?" said Stick.

"It's not exactly a rope," said George, pulling out the tights. His face was pale pink under the plaster.

Tub hooted, "You're going to let Julia know that? She'll have you for breakfast. She told you Sharon would make you wear tights."

"Do you have any better ideas?" said George.

Julia was yelling down at them again.

"There's the door handle. It seems okay."

"Right," said George. "Catch these and tie one end to the handle, then lower the rest back down to us." He threw the tights up and Julia caught them.

"Tights," she crowed. "I told you she'd make you wear them."

George looked at Tub. "One word, just one word."

Tub didn't say it.

A long black thing snaked down toward them.

"I've tied it as tight as I could," said Julia.

George looked at Kev. "You first," he said.

"Why me?" said Kev again.

"Because if it takes *your* weight, it'll take anybody's," said George.

As it turned out, the tights were pretty strong. They weren't the flimsy variety. More what George's mother would have called "winter weight."

"It's like abseiling in reverse," said George to Kev. "You just grab the tights, put your feet on the wall, and walk up."

"I've done abseiling," Kev said.

"I know," said George. "The headmaster knows, the whole school knows about your abseiling."

The only real difficulty was getting started. Every time Kev tried to haul himself up, the tights stretched even further, until they could stretch no more. Once he was safely up, the rest were confident enough to fight over whose turn it was. The only

problem was the dog. George stuffed it down Stick's jacket and zipped up the jacket tightly.

"Climb," he said.

Stick climbed.

At last they all sat on the top landing. George undid the tights from the door handle. The legs seemed to be about three meters long now, but he couldn't help that. Losing the blouse was bad enough without losing the tights as well. For all he knew, they might be family heirlooms too. Maybe they had belonged to her grandmother. There was a sound in the hall below them. They froze. George crept to the head of the stairs.

"It's them," he mouthed.

Nobody moved. He crept back to them.

"Look," he whispered, "the first thing they'll do is look in the closet. If we can get down the stairs while they're doing that, we'll get clean away."

Nods all around.

They listened as the sound of feet crossed the hall.

"Ready to talk yet?" said a voice.

"Original, isn't he?" whispered Tub.

Still silence from the closet.

"Maybe something's happened to them," said Joe.

"Like what?" said Fred. "They're just playing games. Wait till I get my hands on them. Give me the key."

There was the sound of the key turning in the lock, then a muffled yell.

"Look at this."

They would both be in the closet by now, thought George.

"Okay," he whispered, "don't make a sound."

Stick stood up. There was a wriggling inside his jacket and the dog fell out with a thud. It immediately began barking.

"I always said you were too thin," said George to Stick as they threw themselves in a clump at the stairs. Kev took to the banisters. They heard the thud of feet as Fred and Joe came out of the closet like bullets out of a gun. The dog was leaping around their feet in a frenzy of excitement, barking itself silly. The leash wrapped itself around Stick's ankles, and he fell in a welter of arms and legs. The others fell over him.

The only one still in action was Kev. The banisters creaked ominously under his weight as he approached the bottom. Fred made a lunge for him. Kev's arm went out to steady himself and caught Fred just below the ear. It was Fred's bad luck that it was the arm in the cast. He went down like a stone, the banisters gave way, and George, who had been wedged up against them, fell off the stairs into the hall below. He had only a moment to wonder if he was all right before Tub fell on top of him. By this time Joe was at the bottom of the stairs waiting, barring their exit. Fred had begun to groan, so at least he wasn't dead, but he wasn't showing any signs of wanting to get up either. George had a lot of sympathy for that. He felt exactly the same.

One by one they all began to struggle to their feet.

"Right," said Joe. "I've had enough of this. You talk and you talk now."

He stretched out a long arm and grabbed Julia.

"Unless you want her hurt," he said.

For the first time George began to feel angry. Up until now he hadn't taken Fred and Joe seriously—not deep down. But now—well, Julia looked scared, and he hadn't ever seen her look scared before. She might be the world's biggest pest, but she was only a kid.

Stick clambered down beside him, the dog close at his heels. "I wouldn't mind," he said, "but Mom would kill me." He had a funny way of showing it, but he was worried too.

George looked at Julia. Her mouth was clamped shut to stop it from trembling. Joe's face grinned above her. Big lout, thought George, frightening a kid. Some tough guy he was, scared of dogs . . . That was it.

"Give me the rest of the fizz bullets," George hissed to Tub.

"They're for an emergency," said Tub.

George looked at him. "I'd hate to know what you would call an emergency. Hand them over."

"How can you eat candy at a time like this?" whispered Stick as Tub handed it over.

"He's scared of dogs," said George softly.

"Stop mumbling and talk," said Joe.

Fred was beginning to move now. He rolled over on to his stomach.

"What if we set the dog on you?" said George, keeping his eyes on Joe's. His hands opened the paper bag behind his back and the candies dropped to the floor. The dog leapt on them.

"Don't make me laugh," said Joe. "That thing?"

"It might not be very big," said George, "but if you get bitten by a rabid dog, you don't much care what size it is." He moved back.

The dog stood there, grinning stupidly. From its mouth came bubbles of pink foam. There was even some dripping from its lower jaw. George knew it wouldn't fool Joe for long, not once he thought about it, but it might give them long enough. Out of the corner of his eye he could see the carriage the men had wheeled out of the closet. Joe hesitated, his eyes fixed on the dog. His grip on Julia relaxed. George moved.

"Get Julia," he yelled as he lunged for the carriage.

Fred was on all fours by this time. Kev launched himself in a beautiful tackle at Joe. Stick grabbed Julia. Tub scooped up the dog and George was behind the carriage. He pushed it with all he had.

The carriage glanced off Fred as it passed, and he went down again with a thump. Straight as an arrow it made for Joe in the doorway. He dived aside just in time, and the carriage hurtled out onto the drive. George followed it.

"Run," he yelled.

They didn't need to be told. In fact, they were running so hard they nearly ran into the backhoe that was rumbling up the driveway.

"Hey, you kids," said a man in a hard hat. "What are you doing in there? It's dangerous!"

And how, thought George

"You going to demolish it?" he said as a van with DEMOLITION CONTRACTORS on the side drew up behind the backhoe. A couple of men got out.

"That's the idea," said one of them.

"Well, there are two men in there having a fight," said George.

"What?" said the other man. "We'll see about that. You kids get on out of here."

The driver of the backhoe climbed down. George looked back in time to see him lay a heavy hand on Joe's shoulder as he appeared in the doorway.

"That'll give us a bit of breathing space," he said. "Come on."

Julia was beginning to look better.

"Thanks, George," she said as they trundled off across the common.

"Don't mention it," said George. "Your mom

would have killed Stick if anything had happened to you. Anyway, it was Tub's idea really."

"What?" said Tub.

"That time when you said about frightening people with a rabid dog," said George. "I remembered it. Great idea."

Tub looked at him to see if George was making fun of him. He didn't seem to be.

"I got it out of a comic," said Tub.

George grinned.

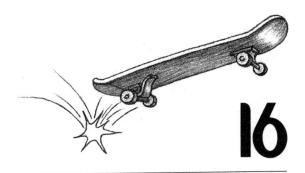

16

Tell you one thing," said Tub. "I'll be glad to get home. I'm starving."

"We're not going home," said George.

"I am," said Tub. "I want my dinner."

"You've missed it," said George. "Look at the time. If we hurry, we'll just make the concert."

"You're not seriously thinking of going to the concert now," said Stick. "After what we've been through? Look at us."

They were a sorry sight, bedraggled and covered in plaster dust, but George was determined.

"If we don't make that concert, we'll never hear the end of it. Now, here's the plan."

They all groaned.

"I don't think I can stand the strain," said Tub.

"You're just scared of Sharon," said Julia.

Gratitude didn't last long with her.

George ignored them. "We go through the park," he said, "swap the cherub and the gnome again, and take the gnome to the school. Then when the concert's over we explain everything to Mr. Martin and get him to take it to the police."

"Why don't we just take it to the police now?" said Kev.

"Because we don't have time," said George. "Can you imagine how long it would take to explain, and besides, I can't think of anybody else that would listen to us. It might take a while to get him to believe us, but at least he'll listen."

"My social worker would listen," said Kev.

"Okay," said Tub, "so long as we go past McDonald's."

"First we've got to get the gnome back," said George.

It wasn't easy, but they managed it. The cherub was listing slightly to one side by the time they had gotten it back. It looked drunk. They all got splashed with water, which made the plaster congeal in horrible lumpy bits, but nobody was bothered much.

They pooled their resources and managed three Big Macs and an order of fries for the dog among them. There was some trouble getting served because of the way they looked. George explained that they were made up for a play they were doing at school. The woman behind the counter smiled.

"Oh, yes, my Amanda's in that," she said. "I'm hoping to get there later myself. She's in the ballet scene, but she hurt her knee roller-skating. I hope she'll manage all right."

George smiled. Amanda and his roller skates. Life wasn't all bad.

They went in by the back door. The first person they saw was Mr. Martin.

"Thank goodness you're here," he said. "Sharon's been jumping around like a cat on hot bricks."

Then he really looked at them.

"Where have you been? And what's the carriage for?"

George opened his mouth to start to explain, but Mr. Martin waved him aside.

"Never mind. It's probably something I don't want to hear anyway. Now, are any of you in the choir?"

Stick owned up. "Sharon says I'm a baritone," he said.

"That's one of the nicer things she says about you," said Mr. Martin. "Well, get onstage. The curtain is about to go up. And get cleaned up, the rest of you."

Stick bounced off, and Mr. Martin disappeared to have a word with the pianist. The rest looked at each other.

"Mr. Martin will listen to us," mimicked Julia.

"There's no justice in the world," said Tub.

"You go and get changed," said George. "I'll wait here with the gnome."

The other three were in the next act—a Native American ballet. Kev was playing the bongo drum. It had been pointed out to him that bongos weren't Native American, but he wasn't easy to reason with. Julia was doing her rotten ballet and Tub was to be tied to a stake in the middle of the stage. He had seemed quite happy about it till they told him it wasn't that kind of steak. Luckily Sharon was also in the ballet, being a beautiful maiden. She was supposed to rescue Tub. In fact, Sharon was in everything. She had worked out a complicated costume-change routine. It would have done justice to a professional, but it didn't leave her much time between scenes.

George hid behind the carriage as the choir came offstage. He saw Sharon fly past to get her costume on, then Stick appeared. He looked as if he needed cheering up.

"Were you singing the same song as everybody else?" said George, and Stick thumped him and looked better.

Julia, Tub, and Kev arrived dressed for their act.

They had managed to get some of the plaster off, but the general effect was a covering of pale mud.

"They'll think it's makeup," said George.

"Never mind that," said Julia. "You'll never guess who we've just seen out in back."

"The TV people," George groaned.

"No, they're out front," said Julia. "It was Fred and Joe."

"How would they know we were here?" said George, stunned.

"The concert got good publicity, remember?" said Julia. "What are we going to do?"

"I *really* hate that question," said George. The dancers were beginning to take their places onstage.

"Take the gnome," said George.

"Where?" said Tub.

"Onstage," said George. "Right out in the open."

Stick groaned. "Not again. It's the same plan, you know. Can't you think up anything new?"

"No," said George. "Can you?"

Silence all around.

"Just put it in the middle of the stage, Kev."

"That's where I'm supposed to be," said Tub.

"Well, you won't be. I'll need you," said George.

"But that means Sharon will have to rescue the gnome. She'll go mad," said Julia, grinning.

"You don't dance in this thing, do you, Tub?" said George.

"No, I just stand there," said Tub.

"No problem, then," said George. "That's what statues are good at—standing there."

There were hisses from the stage.

"You'd better get going," said George as Sharon appeared.

She looked at George in horror. "What on earth have you been doing, George? You'd better get cleaned up and changed. We're on next, you know. And I hope you know your lines. Where were you this afternoon anyway?"

George muttered something, but she wasn't listening.

"Come along," she said to the others, and swept out onto the stage. Kev hefted the gnome and staggered after her, closely followed by Julia, grinning broadly. There was just time to see the surprise on the dancers' faces as Kev plonked the statue down in the middle of the stage. Then the music began and the curtain went up.

"Come on, Tub," said George.

"Where to?" said Tub.

"I want you to find Mr. Martin. Tell him everything. I don't care if he doesn't have time to listen. Sit on him if you have to, but tell him."

"What about me?" said Stick.

"You stay here. Make sure that gnome doesn't come off the stage for anything—anything at all."

"What are you going to do?" said Tub.

"Keep them away from the stage," said George.

He grabbed the carriage. "Now get going."

One thing the council had done when they built the school—they had given it a really professional stage. There was some idea that it would be a community theater. So it had the works, a curtain that went up and down, backdrops, flies, all of it. George made his way carefully toward the corridor at the back of the stage. He saw Fred and Joe almost at once, and they saw him.

I'll have nightmares about this for years, he thought as he made off in the other direction. From the stage he could hear Kev pounding away on the bongo drum. He slewed around a corner and found what he was looking for, the stairs that led under the stage. If he could get them down there and lock them in, they'd be safe. He left the door open deliberately as he bumped the carriage downstairs. They would have to come down after him. If he could hide till they'd gone down the far end, he could get back up the stairs and jam something against the door.

It was dark below the stage. Above him, feet thudded rhythmically. He picked his way through the boxes, ropes, and props that littered the floor. From the head of the stairs—nothing. Surely they must have seen the open door. The dancing above seemed to be coming to a crescendo.

For the first time it occurred to George that he was on next. What was the point anyway? He had no costume, he was covered in plaster dust and stuck under the stage. He pulled out the tights. It was good to be prepared anyway, he thought. They were so long and thin by this time, he had a lot of difficulty getting them on. And even when he pulled them right up to his chest, there was still about a meter flapping at the end of his feet.

There was a burst of applause from above. It drowned out the sound of Fred and Joe coming down the stairs. It was only when Fred fell over something and swore that George realized he had company. It wasn't surprising Fred had bumped into something. The floor was covered with stuff. George had found one of the few clear places. He scrambled to his feet as quickly as he could, cursing the dangling ends of the tights. It wasn't going to be easy running in them, and he was going to miss his scene in any case. The applause had died down now. By this time Sharon would be half into her Juliet costume. All in all he was beginning to feel it was far better if he didn't appear. There were more crashing noises from the other end of the room.

"See if you can find a light switch, Fred," said Joe. "It's black as pitch down here."

"You sure he came down here?" said Fred.

"Where else could he have gone?" said Joe. "Just look for a switch, will you?"

George stood still. In the dark it wasn't easy to

place them, and he didn't want to run straight into them. At least he knew the direction the stairs were in. When they found the light switch, he'd make a dash for the stairs while the light was still blinding them. He heard a muffled voice from above announcing the next act, then Fred's voice. "I've found a switch."

George tensed.

"Don't just stand there," said Joe.

There was the sound of a switch being thrown, and George felt the ground tremble beneath him. He thought briefly of earthquakes, then, unbelievably, he felt the floor rise under him. He staggered slightly. There was a dazzling light above him as the stage seemed to open up.

As he ascended, blinking in the light, he heard yells from below him closely followed by a great burst of laughter. He looked at the audience in dismay and then at his feet as the trapdoor closed over the ends of the tights. Trapdoor, sure enough, he thought. He tried to move. No good. He was caught. The audience had begun to applaud. He turned away. The first thing he saw was the gnome, center stage, grinning evilly at him. The next was Sharon. She was standing on a raised balcony thing and her expression was worse than the gnome's.

"What do you think you're doing?" she whispered.

"I'm stuck in the trapdoor," said George.

"Where's your costume? You look ridiculous."

"I'm wearing the tights," said George.

He looked down at his legs. She was right. He shouldn't have put them on over his jeans. The applause had died down. The audience waited expectantly.

"Get on, then," Sharon urged him.

George's mouth went dry. He suddenly couldn't remember a word of his speech. Shakespeare, he thought. Sharon was tapping her foot.

George spoke. "'Ill met by moonlight, proud Titania,'" he yelled. Then he dried up completely.

The audience roared.

"That's the wrong play," said Sharon. "Will you do it right or get off."

George looked at his feet. Short of taking the tights off, he was stuck. He couldn't remember a line of what he was supposed to say. He looked wildly at the sides of the stage. Surely somebody had the script. What he saw froze his blood. On one side Fred, on the other Joe, just waiting for the curtain to come down.

George made up his mind. He turned to the audience and for the first time saw the TV cameras. That did it. Nothing in his entire life could be worse than this. He looked at the audience. The audience looked back at him—expectantly.

"I'm fed up," he said to the sea of faces. "Just fed up. I've been locked in the Sports Center, locked in a closet, and now I'm caught in this trapdoor and all because of that gnome."

He pointed at it. A smattering of laughter came from the audience. He turned on them, furious.

"You may think it's funny," he yelled. The laughter spread. "But I don't," he went on. "I knew it would be like this. I knew nobody would believe a word of it." He could hear Sharon making squeaking noises behind him, but he plunged on. "Can't you just listen for a minute?" he roared at the audience. Some of them began to clap, and George realized with a sickening feeling that they thought it was part of the show.

"This is real," he yelled, dancing around in his agitation.

The tights, held firm in the trapdoor, pulled him off balance and he fell to his knees. There was more applause, and he looked up and found the eye of the TV camera staring at him from the back of the auditorium. He got slowly to his feet. The applause ended. He tried to keep calm.

"Look," he said. "This is not part of the show." He pointed again at the gnome. "That," he said, "is the statue that was stolen from the museum. The one that's been in the papers . . ."

He waited a moment to let the audience get a good look at it. There was a flurry at the sides of the stage, and out of the corner of his eye he saw Fred and Joe disappear.

"Surely some of you must recognize it. Somebody must have been to the museum. Its picture was in the paper," he said desperately.

There was a murmur among the audience as they craned their necks to get a better look. At least they had stopped laughing. There was a crash and a thud and Fred and Joe appeared from either side of the stage and ran up the center aisle, making straight for the TV camera.

"That's them," yelled George. "They're the ones who stole it."

There was another scatter of laughter and a few whoops from some of the audience. George groaned. Maybe it was a defect in his personality. Maybe he was doomed to go through life not being taken seriously. Well, it wasn't his fault. Nobody could say he hadn't tried.

Tears of frustration stood in his eyes, so he couldn't see who it was that jumped up out of a seat in the third row and began to shout. It looked like a demented dwarf.

"That's them. That's the kidnapers I told you about, Jenny. Get them, somebody."

Immediately there was pandemonium. People were out of their seats. Children were yelling. It was real audience participation.

The last thing George saw as the curtain came down was the headmaster sitting in the front row with his head in his hands.

"I'll never forgive you for this, George Aitken," said a voice behind him.

George twisted around in time to see Sharon's face as she climbed over the balcony. It rocked slightly under her weight and gently folded up. George ripped the tights off and was running before she got to her feet.

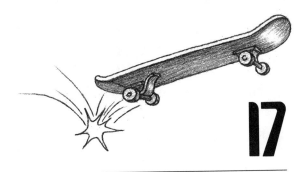

The auditorium was quiet. The audience had gone home. There was none of this stuff about the show must go on. The show was wrecked and everybody knew it. The TV crew was happy enough. They went away saying things like "great television" and "human drama," even though the police had impounded their film. They said it was evidence. Fred and Joe hadn't been caught, but the inspector said not to worry. As far as he understood, it was all on film and they would have no trouble identifying them.

The curator of the museum had been called and, after thanking the group, had personally seen to the crating of the gnome. He fussed over it till he got it out of the building and into the van that was to take it to the police station. It was evidence too.

Mr. Martin and Jenny had explained to Jenny's aunt that there had never been a baby and had taken her home.

"Hi, Kev," Jenny had said. "Turning into a solid citizen at last? I had a word with your mother earlier and she says she's not having a patio after all. Something tells her it's not meant to be. She thinks your wild garden will be more restful." Kev had looked embarrassed.

"That's my social worker," he said to George.

Sharon had gone home after an interview with the TV people. She had a few pointed words to say to George about the return of the velvet vest and the antique blouse.

"You can keep the tights," she said generously.

"Thanks a bundle," said George. He was through with Sharon Taylor.

Finally only the headmaster was left. He looked at them sadly. "I don't quite know what to say," he said, but he carried on anyway. "I don't doubt that you have all done very well in getting the museum's statue back. Indeed, the curator was telling me it's the only really valuable piece the museum possesses. An early Corinthian figure of the Greek god Pan, as I understand. However, I cannot help but feel that the cost has been considerable."

Too right, thought George. All that percentage money. He would never get the skateboard now.

The headmaster's arm swept around the auditorium. Rows of seats were overturned and on the stage bits of scenery bulged through the curtain. From under a chair came a faint yelp and the dog slunk out.

"Nevertheless," the head went on, "only a few people asked for their money back. Most seemed to enjoy the entertainment. In fact, one or two said it was the best show they had seen in years. So I think I shall have to let it go at that."

There was a roar from the entrance, and Mr. Hughes, the janitor, appeared.

"What's all this, then? Turn my back on the place for five minutes and this happens. All I did was go out for a quiet pint. Well? Who's going to clean it up, then? That's what I want to know."

The headmaster vanished so quickly, George looked around for another trapdoor.

It was a full hour before they had the place cleaned up to the janitor's satisfaction and he let them go.

"It's not fair," said Julia. "You'd think we would get more thanks than that."

"The guy from the museum was pretty pleased," said Tub.

"Do you think we'll get the reward?" said Stick.

George winced. "Reward? That would be a laugh

with our luck. Do you realize we haven't made a penny on this? The concert proceeds were our last chance and we didn't get near them all night."

"Imagine that gnome being valuable," said Kev. "What's a Pan?"

"Oh, shut up, Kev," said the rest, and the dog bit him on the ankle.

They were called in to the headmaster first thing Monday morning. The inspector was there. So was the curator of the museum. The headmaster coughed.

"You'll be glad to know that the two men involved in the theft have been caught," he said.

"Once we had the TV film, it was a snap," said the inspector. "They've been in trouble before but nothing as big as this. I've just been telling your headmaster we need more youngsters like you."

George could see the thought of more youngsters like Kev haunting Mr. Redfeather.

The curator was speaking. "I understand you have also been raising money for school equipment. Very commendable, I must say. It's good to see children doing this sort of thing. There are too many people ready to condemn youngsters without—"

Julia couldn't stand the strain.

"Do we get the reward?" she said.

He looked as if he would like to condemn her.

"Of course," he said. "I have it here and I shall be very happy to divide it among you, but first I must just say a few words. . . ."

He went on for ages, but finally he had to hand over the money. They stood there clutching the crisp notes. Tub remembered to say thank-you, and the rest chimed in as well. They could hardly wait to get out.

"I might get a drum kit," said Kev. "I really enjoyed those bongos."

Tub was wondering if you could buy a season ticket for McDonald's.

"What are you going to spend yours on, George?" said Stick.

George stared at him.

"What do you think? The skateboard, of course."

What a question!

"I'm going to get it at lunchtime before somebody changes their mind about the reward."

But first he had to go and get Sharon's blouse back.

"Here's your eight pounds," he said to the man in the antiques shop. "I'll have that blouse back."

The man picked it up and pointed to the ticket. Ten pounds, it said.

"But it was only eight we owed you," said George, "for that thing we broke."

The man leaned across the counter.

"Look, son," he said, "I've got a business to run.

Overhead, taxes, wear and tear. I can't sell at the price I buy. It's not business. Everybody's got to make their percentage."

George handed over a ten-pound note. He couldn't argue with economics. After all, it was what he had been preaching to the rest.

He had to wait until after school to go for the skateboard. He could feel it under his feet as he raced to the store. The swoop of it, the speed, the smooth-running wind-rushing flight of it.

He was out of breath by the time he reached the store. For a minute he stood looking at the skateboard in the window. Then, as he looked at it, it turned into a vacuum cleaner. He rubbed his eyes and it was a skateboard again. *I must be cracking up*, he thought, and he pushed open the door.

"I want to buy the vacuum cleaner in the window," he said to the shopkeeper, and a horrible cold, slimy feeling came over him.

The woman looked at him as if he were mad.

"You're in the wrong store, dear. Next door at the electrician's."

George couldn't believe it was happening. It was not like him. It just *was not* George Aitken. Even when he found himself next door at the electrical shop handing over all that lovely money for a

second-hand vacuum cleaner—a *vacuum cleaner*—
he still couldn't believe it.

It was even worse when he got home.

"But, George, it was your reward money."

His mother was pleased. You could tell by the way
she was talking to him—accusing him.

"What made you do it?"

"I don't know," said George miserably.

She smiled then. "Come on and have your dinner," she said. "You can try the vacuum cleaner out
on the weeds later."

What was worrying George more than anything
was what he was going to tell the rest of the gang
when he turned up without the skateboard. He
couldn't tell them he had bought a vacuum cleaner.
He couldn't think what had come over him. He
broke out in a cold sweat picturing their faces. As for
what Julia would say . . . He wondered if he was old
enough to emigrate.

They made the evening news that night. The police
had released the film. George saw Sharon being
sweet about "the social responsibilities of young
people today," then the film cut to Fred and Joe tear-
ing up the aisle. He could see himself in the background with his mouth open and the tights stuck in
the trapdoor.

His mother came into the room.

"How did you manage with that fund-raising?" she said.

George scowled. "I'm finished with fund-raising," he said. "I don't think I'm cut out for business."

"Fund-raising isn't business, it's charity," she said.

George opened his mouth to say something uncharitable about charity, but she was still talking.

"Did you get your package?" she asked.

George looked up, surprised.

"What package?"

"I left it in your room. It came today but with the vacuum cleaner and all, I forgot about it."

"I haven't been up there yet," said George.

He wondered who on earth could be sending him packages. He never got packages. Then, when he saw the oblong box lying on his bedroom floor, he thought—oh, rats, they've sent me a plastic replica of the gnome for a memento.

But it wasn't. He ripped the paper off and there lay a box with a picture on it and inside the box, the real thing. It looked a million times better than Sharon Taylor. A letter fluttered out and he read it through quickly. He looked from it to the skate-board lying in its wrapping paper. He couldn't believe it. He'd won the contest—the mug's game. He had even forgotten he'd entered it.

Parts of the letter jumped out at him "congratulations," "most original name," "most entries Star Wars—type names," "makes a really eye-catching label."

He looked at the skateboard again. *His* skateboard. And he wouldn't have to tell the rest about the vacuum cleaner.

On one corner was a picture of a rearing horse with feathery things sticking out of its sides.

"Mom," he yelled. "I've won the contest. I've won the skateboard."

His mother came to the bottom of the stairs.

"What?"

"I've won. They're going to use my name for the skateboard."

She looked puzzled.

"What—George?"

He was hanging over the banisters.

"No, Pegasus."

"And who's Pegasus when he's at home?"

George's voice rang through the house.

"A mythical winged horse," he shouted. "We did it in classical background."

His mother's face broke into a smile.

"See what I've always told you about studying," she said.

But George was downstairs and out the door before she had finished speaking.

He launched himself down the street on the skateboard. His voice floated on the air as he whizzed around the corner, arms outstretched on either side of him—like wings.

"*Pe—ga—sus*," he yelled as he flew.

About the author

Helen McCann wrote *What Do We Do Now, George?* in tribute to her father, who made her laugh with the stories he told her as a child, to writers who made her laugh as a young reader, and to her children, now teenagers, who have always been able to make her laugh, too. She hopes the book will do the same for the children who read it. It is her first novel. It is not a serious book.

Helen McCann lives in Scotland.

About the illustrator

Ellen Eagle has illustrated many novels and picture books including the Magic Mysteries by Elizabeth Levy and *Tales of Tiddly* by Dolores Modrell.

She and her husband live in Glen Ridge, New Jersey.